LOST HUNTRESS

NICHOLAS WOODE-SMITH

Contents

Chapter 1.   Nightkin 5

Chapter 2.   MonsterHunter 16

Chapter 3.   Friendship 22

Chapter 4.   Welfare 38

Chapter 5.   Drakenbane 54

Chapter 6.   Conspiracy 67

Chapter 7.   Eviction 73

Chapter 8.   Ghosts 80

Chapter 9.   Where I belong 84

Chapter 10.   First Blood 93

Chapter 11.   Clientele 108

Chapter 12.   A Bridge Too Far 127

Chapter 13.   Agency 150

Chapter 14.   Friend Far Away 160

Chapter 15.   Demons 174

Chapter 16.   Far from Home 190

Chapter 17.   Entrepreneurship 203

Chapter 18.   The Big Leagues 219

Chapter 19.   Perspective..251

Chapter 20.   Saviour..264

Chapter 21.   Conspiracy..269

Chapter 22.   Vendettas 282

Chapter 23.   Into the Darkness...................................296

Chapter 24.   Death..305

Chapter 25.   Life...323

Afterword...326

Acknowledgements 327

Chapter 1. Nightkin

Always get paid upfront.

A lot can happen to a client before the mission is done. They could skip town. Disappear, intentionally or accidentally. Things can change. The economy is unpredictable, after all. There are a thousand and one different things that can go wrong at any given time.

But, we don't all have the benefit of being able to negotiate with our clients. And, without Conrad Khoi, my agent that turned out to be an angel (now ex-angel and ex-agent), I didn't really have the bargaining power I once did.

But, at least I still had my pixie.

"Get down here, ya flamin' ball bag!" Duer yelled at the nightkin, looming on a tree branch just above us.

"I don't think it can speak pixie," I added, rolling my eyes while resisting a grin. I shouldn't encourage him.

"All monsters speak the same language," Duer replied. "Isn't that right, ya shitey bugger?"

"And what language is that?" Treth asked.

"Treth asks what language that is."

"Tell ye split personality, Maddy," he chided, grabbing onto my hair to steady himself on my shoulder. "That monsters know two things: curses and steel."

"Sometimes silver," I added.

"Yes! Sometimes silver."

The nightkin growled at us, a low bellow that vibrated the tree and crackled like fire. It had been a long time since I had fought a nightkin. In fact, my first paid bounty had been for a nightkin. They looked like monkeys with vampiric teeth, wreathed in grey flames, with a pair of flaming coal-like orbs for eyes. They were also one of the more puzzling monster types. They were neither undead, spirit nor vampire, but all three simultaneously. It was very confusing.

And fighting them wasn't much better. Nightkin were fast. Too fast a lot of the time. It's why most agencies didn't hunt them. Not that they were dangerous. Agencies fought drakes and trolls on a regular basis. It's just that nightkin were the violent pests of the magical world. They needed to be removed, but nobody was willing to go through the trouble of removing them. Couldn't just mow them down. They anticipated the bullets. And even mages struggled to send magical ordinance their way. If a nightkin didn't want to fight, they knew how to stay away.

So, what is a swordswoman like me meant to do?

"Come face ye death, ya ape-faced bastard!"

The nightkin's eyes flickered as it peered at me from its vantage. I heard the deep rumble of its growl.

Duer glowed as he smirked. He was having fun.

"Why did you bring the pixie along, anyway?" Treth asked. It's not that he disliked Duer. In fact, Treth admired a lot about the tenacious pixie. But Treth had been in a bad mood for a while. Since I befriended a necromancer, swapped eyes with her, and channelled her magic to raise a zombie, to be precise.

Can't say I blamed him for his anger. If I was to tell my past self of what I had done, I'd probably have slapped myself with the flat of my sword. But my past self hadn't met Candace. Hadn't gotten to know that behind the Necrolord was a fragile girl who had lost her parents. I had seen the humanity in the necromancer and had not only been unable to defeat her but wanted to embrace her.

Yet, Candace's grand scheme to bring back her parents had failed. I feared that she was broken by that. And I was unsure of what would win out in the war within her head. The dark or the light. At least I knew there was no longer any madness. My connection to her through her eye in my head made that clear. Past that, I didn't know what she was doing. I wasn't a necromancer. And didn't want to be despite what Treth may think. But that meant I couldn't reliably control what I saw of Candace's life. Just glimpses. Uncontrolled and random.

I sensed Duer about to open his mouth to taunt the nightkin again when I heard a distinct hum. I bent my knees and readied my short-swords – loans from Brett until I bought new ones for myself. They were robust designs. Not as swift as I would have liked, but they'd go through flesh and bone easily enough.

"Get ready," I commanded Duer, who swallowed his oncoming insult.

The nightkin blinked out of existence, not even leaving a puff of smoke. I heard traffic in the distance and birds chirping in the dying afternoon light. The leaves rustled as a gust of wind passed through them.

I took a step back.

Poof.

The nightkin appeared behind me. Duer jumped, gliding away to safety as I spun. A claw of ever-burning fur and flesh came my way. It didn't seem to care about the flames of my coat. It did seem to mind the cold bite of steel, however, as I brought up my off-hand blade, slicing off the tips of its fingers. It wailed, it's unearthly cry echoing around the suburb. I brought my other sword in a swift arc towards it. Not swift enough! It blinked away.

"Too slow," Treth chided.

"Of course, too fucking slow," I bit back at him. "Have you seen these metal slabs?"

"Front."

"What?"

The wind shot out of me as I fell backwards, kicked by a blur of grey that appeared just in front of me. I tried to regain my footing and felt Duer pushing the back of my head to keep me steady. Wasn't good enough and I fell on my backside with a thud.

I slashed out wildly, anticipating that the nightkin would go in for the kill. It didn't.

"Come out and fight us like men!" Duer yelled.

"Shut him up," Treth said. "I'm trying to think."

"He's the bait. He's meant to keep speaking."

"Wait…" Duer trailed off. "Bait…?"

The nightkin reappeared in a blink behind the pixie. I kicked myself off the ground and swatted Duer out of the way with the knuckle of my left hand, while driving my right-hand sword into the nightkin's chest.

It let out a sputter and a fiery wheeze, and then its flames went out and all that was left was a grotesque monkey-creature, with hollow eyes. I let its body fall to the ground

Duer flew up to the beast's head. Kicked it. He glowed a fierce gold and looked up at me.

"No need to thank me," he said, puffing out his chest like a hero on parade.

I suppressed a snicker. Treth was not amused.

I drew my seax, one of my original weapons that I had fortunately not lost in the fires of Candace's stronghold and set about cutting the nightkin's head off. Clients sometimes needed brutal reminders of why they paid us.

Duer considered my work and then my scuffed shoes and dirt-laden pants. I had fallen into a muddy patch.

"You'd fight better if you took that contact out," he said.

I sighed. "For the billionth time, it's not a contact. It's the eye of the Necrolord. We swapped eyes and she disappeared before we could swap back."

He rolled his eyes.

"You think me the fool, eh? Well, joke all you want, but that footwork wasn't you, Maddy. You're much better than that usually."

I frowned, biting back a retort. He was right. I wasn't as good as I used to be. Sloppy. I blamed these new swords. They weren't designed for agile fighting. I also blamed my months in captivity. I was out of form.

But more than that, it was something else. It was as if I didn't feel as in-sync with my mind, my body and my spiritual companion.

I pulled the nightkin's head off, breaking the last bits of bone and skinny tendrils. It didn't stink like normal corpses. Just another thing to add to the confusion of classifying and understanding it.

I shrugged. At least it died like any other creature.

I carried the head through the back garden of this suburban home and went down the side. The client didn't want blood dripping in the house.

The client, a man of middle years with short hair and a cranky demeanour, was waiting out the front, talking to a neighbour. On seeing my approach, the neighbour gasped and beat a hasty retreat. I tended to have that effect on people. And it wasn't just the head in my hand. The new eye and flaming coat didn't help me look *normal*.

I held the nightkin's head aloft until he got a good look at it, then I tossed it into a nearby bin. It went in the first time. I should be a basketball player.

"That'll be $150," I said, taking out my cell phone so I could confirm payment.

He looked at the blood trailing to his backyard and grimaced. He didn't take out his cell phone.

"I checked your credentials while you were back there," he said.

"And?" I gave him my signature death stare, but I must've been tired, as he didn't seem to notice or care.

"You said you were licensed with the MonsterHunter App."

"I am. I signed up to this bounty through the app."

"You aren't on the app."

"What?!"

"I'm sorry," he said, not sounding sorry. "But if you aren't on the app, I can't send you payment."

"I killed the fucking thing!"

"But you aren't registered."

"I was registered!"

"But you aren't now."

"I'll show you!" I looked at my phone and pressed the MonsterHunter App. Loading…Loading…

It wouldn't open.

I restarted my phone and tried to open it again. Nothing. How could this be?

"Miss, here…" he showed me his phone and the bounty file that I had just fulfilled. Under failed applicants was my name. In red. With the words, in all caps: Blacklisted.

Oh, fucking Rifts and Athena.

"H…how?" I managed to choke out.

"I don't know. Or care. But if you aren't a legal hunter, I can't pay you."

"You can pay me cash," I said, a hint of desperation in my voice. "You saw earlier. I was…am…legal. This is just a mix up."

He shook his head.

"Pay her the money, ye bugger," Duer hissed.

"Excuse me?"

"You heard me, you bloated weasel fart! She killed the fecker, so you gotta pay up."

"I don't need to do anything! She's not a legal contractor. The fact that she went into my property under false pretences is grounds for me to call the police!"

I felt a pang of anxiety. I couldn't have that. I wasn't on good terms with the cops after one of their chief inspectors was killed while trying to arrest me. Wrongfully, I might add. And I wasn't the one who killed him. So don't get any wrong ideas.

Duer flew right up to his face and with all the menace his little body could muster, whispered.

"Pay her."

The man tried to swat him out of the way, but Duer deftly evaded the swipe.

"Rifts! I've got half a mind to take up fae dust for this."

"You snort my pixie," I hissed, truly menacing now. "And I'll take your guts as compensation. They'd make good zombie bait."

"Your pixie?" Duer added, affronted.

14

"You threatening me?" the man asked.

I was about to say something I may have regretted when Treth silenced me.

"He's not worth it. It's just one pay check. There'll be others."

"I need that pay check, Treth," I replied.

"Whose Treth?" the man asked, confused and seemingly forgetting about the threat.

I ignored him. "He owes us. And I need to eat. And need new swords."

"You're insane! I'm going to phone the police," he said.

I grabbed his phone from his hands, threw it on the ground and stomped on its screen. I turned on my heel and walked off in a huff.

I thought my biggest issues at the moment were reconciling with Treth and making sure I'd stay fed, but if my license had been revoked, then I had even bigger problems. My entire career as a monster hunter may be over. And I didn't even know why.

Chapter 2. MonsterHunter

"What do you mean you've been blacklisted?" Brett asked over the phone, aghast.

"Fucking client refused to pay me, and my app isn't working."

"Do I need to teach him a lesson?"

"I can fight my own battles, Brett. And we're on thin ice as is."

We weren't exactly on a watch list (actually, we might be), but we were running out of friends in this city. The hunters who had helped me avenge my dead boyfriend all had to go low. The ones who weren't dead, that is. They had careers they needed to defend and murdering a councillor's son wasn't the way to ensure job security. Hammond and the others weren't talking to me. Brett assured me that it wasn't bitterness, but I knew better. I'd led them into a trap. And their friends had died because of it. And what was in it for them?

I needed to repay them for what they had done for me. But before that, I needed to sort out my own life.

"I need to get to the bottom of this," I continued. "If I can't hunt, then…"

I didn't want to fathom it. I'd already dropped out of university. Not like I could afford it on my current income anyway. But if I couldn't hunt, what would I do with my life?

"You should sign up with Drakenbane," Brett suggested. "Don't need a freelance license for that. You will be protected under the agency license."

"I'm not a team player."

"Beggars can't be choosers. And you're great with teams."

"I hate teams."

"I'll choose not to be offended by that. Anyway, hear this: Drakenbane is recruiting again. To replace some losses."

It was left unspoken that some of the losses were my fault.

"I'll put a good word in for you. Guy will as well. It'd be great to have you on board."

"It makes more sense for me to join Puretide."

"Those wusses? Drakenbane's benefits are much better. They recompensate ammunition. Don't have to buy your own."

"I use swords."

"Well, there're other perks as well. But above all…" I could practically see his smirk on the other side. "You'll get to work with me."

"That's more an occupational hazard," I chuckled. "I'll think about it."

Brett replied to someone on the other side.

"Send Guy my love," I said.

"What about me?"

I laughed and hung up.

"This is serious, Kat," Treth said, after I'd stowed my phone away in my jacket pocket.

"Everything is serious with you."

"How was Brett?" Duer asked.

"He's fine. And thanks for the help back there."

He glowed with pride. Seems he didn't mind being bait if the hunt worked out well in the end.

"Because everything these days is serious!" Treth responded.

I stopped walking down the street. Couldn't afford a taxi and someone had stolen my motorcycle while I was interned at Camp Candace.

"Do you think I don't know that?" I whispered. "Do you think I'm blissfully unaware that I'm surviving on instant noodles while my cat has to live with Cindy because I can't afford to feed him? Do you think I want that?"

"You're getting sloppy," was his reply.

I raised my arms in resignation.

"As if that fucking helps, Sir Treth of Concord. Thanks."

He didn't reply and even Duer didn't chime in. I renewed my walk.

"I'm sorry," Treth finally said.

"For fucking what?"

"I don't know."

"I don't know either."

I sighed and leant up against a tree. Duer flew up to the high branches. To look at flowers or whatever.

"We're a fucking mess, aren't we?" I said.

"It's that necro…"

"Candace has fuck all to do with this. This is our problem. Yours and mine."

"What's my problem?" Duer piped up from the tree top.

"Shut up, Duer."

"You shut up."

"You were touched by necromancy, Kat," Treth said. He sounded like he was trying to recite scripture but was failing. His voice was too emotional. These were his words, not the teachings of his long dead masters and friends. "That sort of taint doesn't just go away."

"So, I'm evil now?"

"No…no. Not evil. Never evil, but…"

"Then that settles it. Never evil. I'm fine. Well, my chi or whatever is fine. I'm not tainted by the darkness."

I smiled, trying to disarm him. Failed.

"I still think we should have…"

"Done what?"

He hesitated, but I saw his thoughts, briefly.

Killed Candace.

"She's a sister to me, Treth."

"And that's the problem."

"Treth," I whispered, trying to be diplomatic. "We've been through a lot. But you haven't seen all of it. You didn't see what made me…me."

"I saw my own share of suffering, Kat."

"Exactly, your own share. Not mine. And you don't see what I see through Candace's eye. She's suffering. And I recognise her pain. It's mine."

"If a dog bleeds the same as a human, does it make it human?"

"Stop being so dense."

"Stop making excuses for a necromancer!" he suddenly yelled.

Shocked, I didn't respond. Duer must have felt the tension, despite not even acknowledging Treth's existence. He flew down and hovered in front of me, his little forehead creased with concern.

"We should have killed her," Treth whispered.

I didn't reply. I couldn't. I stood up and made my way home, Duer in tow. Treth and I didn't speak.

Chapter 3. Friendship

I had to kill him. He blocked the way. He knew too much. About who I was. About who I am. If I didn't kill him, he would kill me. I'm sorry, Kat. I didn't want to. I had to. I'm getting better. I swear. I swear. I swear…

***

Candace killed someone.

I didn't see who it was or know why. I couldn't judge if she had been justified or not. I didn't tell Treth, obviously. He wouldn't understand. Especially if I could not. I felt Candace shift between light and dark. Recently, more to the dark. But I felt her sadness. Not madness. And she missed me. But the darkness was still there, tempting her. Speaking to her. I could only watch helplessly, through her eye, as she fought the darkness within.

***

My emails and phone calls to MonsterSlayer App were fruitless. The emails were ignored, and support staff always redirected me to endless jingles by phone. Without being able to reinstate my account, I was unable to get any jobs. No jobs, no money. No money. Sad and hungry Kat. Well, not so much sad as really angry.

What my temporary (hopefully) unemployment meant, besides dreaded idleness, was that it became harder and harder to avoid Trudie. It wasn't like I wanted to avoid her! But I had shown up, practically from the grave, to kill her boyfriend in front of her, just before her boyfriend almost killed her. Perhaps it was unfair that I hadn't seen her in the hospital, but it felt wrong to do so. I was responsible for putting her there. And I couldn't bear facing her after what I had done.

I spoke to Pranish a bit. Not so much about Colin. I didn't speak to anyone about Colin. Not even Treth. I wasn't feeling that close to him as of late. And I needed someone close to talk to. And it was times like these that I wanted my aunt back. But she was probably dead. Like everyone else. Killed by elves. Killed by ANZAC. Didn't matter. She was dead in the crossfire. Yeah, technically missing. But nobody just went missing in the warzone of New Zealand. They died. And their bodies were only ever found in mass graves.

I tried to cry for Mandy. For all I hadn't told her. For all I needed to tell her. But I couldn't. She had been gone too long. She was more an idea than my aunt. I missed her. But

I didn't know who she really was anymore. And now I feared I would never find out.

"Bullseye!" Duer called as I managed to throw some rolled-up scrap paper, ripped from my old history notes, into his birdhouse from across the room.

"What do you need this paper for anyway?"

"Pixie stuff."

"Pixie stuff involving what?"

"Do I ask you about your human stuff?"

"You do, but you accurately don't call it human stuff."

The scrap disappeared further into his house and he reappeared on the lip.

"It isn't the place of lesser beings to ask for explanations from the fae," he replied, haughtily.

I rolled my eyes, but technically he was correct. Fae, even the darned pixies, were higher up on the metaphysical species ladder than humans. The only things that topped them were angels, higher demons, elder dragons and gods. What determined this hierarchy? Many things. Connection to the In Between, relationship to weylines and, appropriately for my purposes, if one could be infected by vampirism or necroblood. Fae could not be turned into vampires by human vampires. But they could be turned into vampires by an Ancient like the one I had banished last year. Vampires could only turn something equal or lower on the totem pole than they. As a human, I was second to the bottom, meaning that almost everything but vampiric squirrels could turn me if I wasn't careful.

Even so, it was hard to take seriously the notion that Duer was cosmically superior to me.

"You should tell Alex that he should respect one of your rank," I chided.

"For ye information, the demonic-feline has become much more agreeable."

"You're getting along with my cat?"

His glow wavered, unsure. "Perhaps not that far…but he hasn't tried to eat me as much."

"Did you two behave at Cindy's?"

"Ye friend of light is a nice lady. Nicer than you. Not that that's hard."

"Hey!"

"But ye cat missed you, Kat."

He snickered at his pun-filled repetition.

"And I missed and miss him."

I frowned. I knew I couldn't afford to keep him, so I left him at Cindy's until I could secure an income. It wasn't fair on him if I couldn't afford to feed him. Duer insisted on tagging along with me. He had survived living in a haunted house for ages, he could survive living with a deadbeat dropout. My words, not his. His were much more colourful.

Duer, bored of the conversation, disappeared into his little house to do the ever-mysterious *pixie stuff*. This left me, once again, idle. And alone, as Treth sulked in his chamber. And let him sulk!

I frowned. Deeper than before, and I looked out my window, at the train tracks and suburbs, stretching into the distance. The window that had been used for bloody messages and for demons from the In Between. I didn't see any people. Just rooftops. A sea of them, yet they also looked lonely.

Snap out of it, Kat!

I slapped my own cheeks.

"I'm a fucking hunter. Act like one."

But I didn't feel like a hunter. I felt like a girl who missed her friends. Who missed her cat. Who missed…everyone. And I was lost.

I took out my cell phone and opened a message from a few days ago. From Pranish.

"Trudie is out of the hospital."

Nothing else. No words of encouragement. No advice regarding what I should do about it. Nothing. And both of them hadn't contacted me since then.

Were they angry? Were they drifting away from me? Or had I pushed them away?

Trudie couldn't change me. She accepted me. Accepted my violence. My incessant knocking on death's door. But I hadn't accepted her. And perhaps, she had had enough.

I sighed, falling to my couch that wasn't there. I fell with an oomph and rubbed my backside. I had forgotten that I had sold the couch to pay the rent. And now more rent was due. Always due. And Ms Ndlovu's kindness could only be stretched so far. I needed a hunt. Not just for my own mind that needed an escape from the drudgery of peaceful life, but because I needed to survive.

But today was not the day for hunts. And Treth was right. I was getting sloppy. My head wasn't in the game. And if I did do a hunt, for no pay, I'd probably lose my head. For no pay.

I stared at Pranish's message. For what seemed like an hour. I heard the crinkle of the paper I had given Duer. And his sing-song humming. I watched the flowers outside grow in real-time as his magical song encouraged them to live.

I stood up from the floor and dusted myself off. I reached for my old leather jacket, but my Salamander coat next to it flared at my approach and I couldn't say no to it. I put it on and left without saying goodbye.

"Where are we going?" Treth asked.

"Back from the dead?"

"Hardly. We find a job?"

"No. But there's something I have to do."

"Trudie?"

I nodded.

"Good luck." He disappeared back into his chamber.

Good luck.

I gulped. I was going to need it.

***

"Kat! We've missed you," Charne Davison, Trudie's mother, almost yelled in joy as she opened the front door. Before I could say anything, she engulfed me in a tight hug that I could not break nor wanted to.

I hesitated, and then hugged her back. I had hurt her daughter. But in her arms, I felt like her daughter. But she was not my mom.

"I missed you too. All of you," I whispered.

She stepped back and indicated for me to enter. The house was just like the last time I had entered it. Albeit less untidy. The last time I was here, I had been with Colin. And Andy had been alive. And then I killed him.

Yet, it didn't bring Colin back.

"You were gone for so long. We were so worried," Charne said. "Missed Christmas, even. And it was Trudie's first Christmas with…"

She paused. Considered her words. Her smile disappeared, for a second, but then reappeared, looking much more forlorn.

"It's good to see you again, Kat."

"Is Trudie home? Pranish said she got out of the hospital."

"She didn't tell you?" Charne asked, bemused.

I fidgeted with my pocket lip.

"Trudie and I…we haven't been fighting, but…it's been a while. You know?"

I looked up at her, squarely in the eyes. It was time to be sincere. Time to say what I wanted. I couldn't keep hiding from my feelings and my friends forever.

"But I want to make amends. She's my best friend. And I need her to know that."

"Kat…Trudie's left the country."

"What? When? Where?"

"Two days after she got out of the hospital. After what happened to…she needed to have some space. She's staying with family in the Thirteen States."

"Why…why didn't she tell me?" the question came out the meekest I'd ever said anything.

Charne put the kettle on and carefully pulled me to sit down on a chair in the kitchen.

"When we took you in," she said, quiet, measured. "We didn't know what you had gone through. And we knew we couldn't know. We were worried. So worried that you wouldn't cope. That you would be lost to us. We didn't think we could ever handle looking after you. After what had happened. But…you became more than friends with Trudie. You became sisters. And you fought and you played. And, I hope you feel the same way, we became a family. And when you finally left us to find your own way, I cried. But I also smiled. Because I knew that you had survived. And that the baby that my best friend showed to me twenty years ago was still there and could still smile."

She stopped, as she stared into the void. She smiled, but her eyes were sad. The kettle whistled and she took it off the stove and poured. Coffee for me. The way I like it. She remembered. She sat down opposite me.

"Kat…Trudie has left us. To go her own way. The same way you did. And as much as that upsets Mike and me, and you, she needs us to let her go. Only she can find her way. And I hope, like you, that she figures out how to beat this."

I looked down at my coffee and didn't reply. Couldn't reply.

I felt Charne cup my hand. I looked up and realised there were tears in my eyes.

"She will come back to us, Kat."

She had a slight sob in her voice, and I saw her eyes glistening with unshed tears.

I reached over the table, spilling the coffee, and put my arms around Charne's neck and cried. She let me as her hand held the back of my head and I wept a torrent of tears, wetting her shirt and neck. She held me as best she could. For a long time. Until my crying turned to dry sobs and sniffling.

"I'm so glad you came back to us, Kat," she said, her voice breaking.

I don't remember making it to the couch, but there we cried together. Her for the hurt of her daughter. Me for what I had done to Trudie. My neglect of my friends. For Colin who wasn't coming back. For Candace fighting her demons. For Treth whom I feared hated me. And for myself. Because I missed my mom, and I loved Charne. But she wasn't my real mom, and never could be. And every bit of love she gave me made me sadder, because it should have been my mom giving it to me. But it never would be.

***

Pranish arrived later that night. Since his disinheritance, he needed a place to stay. And the Davisons were always the home of the homeless. And with Trudie gone, I'm sure they wanted to fill their vacant rooms.

Pranish found me with puffy eyes, now dry, eating dinner and avoiding telling Mike Davison the truth about Candace's eye.

"Freak magical accident," I said.

"It makes you look like a husky," he snickered.

"Don't be rude, Mike," Charne said, putting more food on my plate.

"Thank you! But I can't have all of it."

"You aren't. And you're all skin and bones. What have you been eating?"

Nothing.

"Enough," I lied.

The door opened and we all turned to see Pranish enter. He stopped as he saw me. Charne, blessed woman, refused to allow any awkwardness.

"How was the presentation, Prani?"

I almost spat my potatoes out at Pranish's old nickname.

"It went well, Mrs Davison. Hey, Kat."

I nodded and mouthed a greeting.

Pranish sat down and we continued eating together. Pranish had been continuing with DigiLaw. It wasn't being marketed just yet, but he was currently in the process of establishing a division at UhuruTech, his parents' biggest competitor. To be fair, he wasn't really betraying them. They disinherited him before he approached their enemy. He kept promising throughout the meal to repay the Davison's for their hospitality once he could. Charne kept refusing the offer.

Eventually, with the fullest belly I'd had in a while, I insisted that I needed to go.

"To feed my pixie," I said, and it wasn't really a lie. Duer got cranky when he was hungry. But more because I felt a tension in the air with Pranish.

After successfully insisting on my leaving, I made my way to the door, and stopped just as Charne said.

"Pranish, why don't you give her a lift?"

I was just about to argue when he replied.

"Sure thing. Let's go, Kat."

We made our way outside to where Pranish's car was parked.

"They let you keep the car?" I asked.

"Eventually," he said, a coldness in his voice. "I bluffed and said that I'd uncover their tax evasion if they took away the apartment and car. Only half worked."

"Pranish…"

He opened the door with a sharp forceful pull. I took the hint and got in.

We drove for a few minutes but it seemed an eternity, when he stopped the car and pulled over. I avoided eye contact.

We sat in silence for a while longer, as cars sped past us. I was about to speak when Pranish began, loudly.

"Why the fuck didn't you come?"

"Pranish..." I whispered, almost meekly.

"Why didn't you visit her? Why didn't you speak to her? Why did you ignore my messages?" he yelled.

He looked at me, tears in his eyes.

"Why didn't you stop her from leaving?"

"I...I didn't know."

"Neither did I! I woke up one morning and she was gone. Left her parents a note. Said she was going to visit her cousins in America. But you know what? I looked for the flight records. Broke some laws. And you know what I found?"

He paused, as if I'd know the answer.

"She didn't go to fucking America," he finally continued. "She's still in Hope City."

"Why? Why would she do that?"

"I don't know," he said, angrily. "Maybe it's because you killed her boyfriend right in front of her!"

"That monster killed Colin!"

"And did killing him bring Colin back?"

"No, it fucking didn't!" I yelled back. "But I did it anyway. Because that's what I do. I kill monsters."

"And how many monsters do you have to kill to bring Trudie back for us?"

"I GOT HER BACK BEFORE!"

The volume of my voice brought a silence to the car. Or was it that I'd smashed a dent in his dashboard?

"I'll do it again," I whispered. "I have to."

"Are you really the right person to do that, Kat?" he hissed. "After all you've done? After all you've made me and her see?"

He shook his head. "Maybe Trudie was right. This life of yours…it isn't compatible with…with us."

I unbuckled my seatbelt and opened the door, despite being on a busy road.

"Thank you for the lift. I'll pay you back for the dashboard. Eventually."

He grunted.

"And you know what, Pranish? She didn't watch me do it. That fucker knocked her so hard I thought she'd died. And then I killed him for that. And everything else. And then I saved her life. Again. And I'll do it again. I always do."

I slammed the door shut. He didn't start the car until I was long gone.

Chapter 4. Welfare

Money was tight. MonsterSlayer App still wasn't letting me back on. Duer had even noticed my money trouble and insisted that he'd find his own food. Even then, I scraped together what I could to buy him a jar of honey. Managed to get bread for myself. We shared.

My gun, two rounds of ammunition, and Brett's loaned swords lay idly on the floor of the lounge. There was no more furniture.

I was using my seax to clumsily butter some bread (sold the toaster) when I heard a knock at the door. It interrupted Duer's licking of his fingers and he grabbed a pen to use as a spear.

"I'm pretty sure it's not an enemy, Duer."

"Could be that large lady, asking for money. She's enemy enough."

"Don't be rude. Mrs Ndlovu is nice."

Duer grunted. He disagreed. But it seemed pixies didn't really understand capitalism.

I peered through the eye-hole and saw Brett, hands in his pockets, looking awkward as a dwarf on a basketball court. I opened up.

"Brett? Nice to see you," I tried to sound excited, but he seldom visited me. And he had an awkward way about him right now. It was unusual.

I let him inside.

"Hey, Kat. Hey, Duer."

Duer glowed. He liked Brett. I wondered if he would still like Brett if he knew about his past with the Extermination Corps. I didn't know if Brett had killed any fae, but his fellow Corpsmen definitely had.

"To what do I owe the pleasure of you visiting my lavish manor?"

He peered around at the bare room, with almost everything short of the fridge and a kettle gone.

"I didn't know it was this bad," he whispered, under his breath, but I still heard him.

"I'm still fed. Fit as a fiddle. Just bored. Really bored."

He smirked. "Need some black blood to sate your thirst?"

"Always. Red, sometimes as well. You know me? A little murderess."

"Not so little."

"That an insult?"

"I don't know."

I snorted.

"I'd offer you a place to sit, but the only places left are the counter and my bed."

His smirk grew. "How about the bed?"

"Not today, Brett Callahan. Anyway, what's up?"

He grinned, but I'm not sure at the joke about the bed or my rejection of it.

He reached into his back pocket and withdrew an envelope. He offered it to me. I didn't take it.

"What is this?" I eyed the package sceptically.

"It…it's money. To tide you over. Till things look up."

Brett. Giving me money. My breath caught in my throat.

"I can't accept your money, Brett."

He pushed it into my hands. I pushed it back.

"I won't take your money."

"You need it."

"And I'll earn my own."

"You've been fucked over by MonsterSlayer and back-rent, Kat. None of it is your fault. Take the money."

"And it's not your fault either!"

"But I'm choosing to give it to you."

Why? I wanted to ask.

"It doesn't feel right." I turned my back on him.

"It's a gift, Kat."

"I'd prefer it if it was a loan."

"Then think of it as a loan."

"I know you'd refuse to let me pay you back."

"Kat…there's a time for dignity and a time for survival."

"My survival and dignity are interlinked."

He couldn't reply to that. He understood where I was coming from. Hunters had similar principles.

He sighed. "Well, if you don't take the money, I'm going to have to do other things."

I turned to him, my eyebrows raised. He recoiled, slightly.

"I still can't believe you have the Necrolord's eye."

"Candace's eye," I corrected him.

He approached more closely, and I faced him, crossing my arms.

"If you don't take the money, I'm going to have to buy your groceries for you. And then leave them here."

"I won't eat them."

"I'll make sure they expire quickly." He grinned, wickedly. "So they'll start stinking. And sure, you can keep throwing them out, but with all that waste…with your Scottish surname, you won't be able to bear it. The waste. The lack of frugality. I know you will eventually cave."

I glared at him and he held my stare, until I blinked and he almost laughed, triumphant.

"Good gods, Brett. You're still that irritating agency muscle head."

"But you still love me for it."

"Sure, I do." I sighed. "How about this? You don't give me the money. You don't waste your time shopping and stinking up my apartment. And…I'll sign up to Drakenbane."

"Really?" his eyes lit up like I'd given him a bike for his birthday.

I shrugged. "I may as well. Even if it means seeing your ugly mug all day. At least Guy can keep me company."

"We'll both start writing testimonials! Cindy, too."

"Don't pester them!"

He was already at the door.

"I'll see you tomorrow! I'll book an interview for you for 8am."

"Wait…"

He was gone.

"Well, Treth. It seems we may be able to get back to the hunt."

He grunted his reply.

***

Conrad invited me for a long overdue meeting and meal at the Gravekeeper that evening. It was the first time I'd seen him since James Montague had tried to shoot me in the head and Conrad had revealed that he was an angel. I think. He hadn't told me the details and I hoped to remedy that situation tonight.

"So, do you still have your office?" I asked, making small talk as he showed me to a booth.

"Nah. Gave up the lease. Couldn't afford to renew."

"Where'd all the money I make you end up?" I smirked, but a little bit of it was accusatory.

"Long story."

"Typically, that means you won't tell me."

He shook his head as I sat down.

"No, Kat. I will. And now."

We stopped talking as a waitress came by. Conrad ordered us both a pint of amber ale. He was paying, despite his dwindling funds. At least he wasn't on $0. The waitress left, and I leaned forward, speaking quietly.

"Let's begin, Mr Khoi. And, I hope you'll be telling me the truth. No more acts. No more salesman get-up. You're not my agent anymore. So, you don't need to sell me anything. But I'd like the truth."

He sighed and leant back, speaking normally despite the sensitive nature of the topic.

"My real name isn't Conrad Khoi. Though, I prefer it. Even though it was made due to a misunderstanding. I misheard someone call me comrade? Can you believe it? Well, that was a long time ago."

"What is your real name?"

"Zephon. Of the 56th Host. Bringers of the Last Light. But I haven't called myself that for well over forty years."

"Are you...really an angel?"

"A winged member of the Seraphim? The haughty self-appointed policemen of the realms, the In Between and everything connected to it?"

His expression soured.

"I guess so."

"Guess so? You do realise that this isn't like I discovered you were secretly a fan of a lame boy-band. You're one-short of a god on the metaphysical ladder!"

He waved away the comment.

"And fat use it was for me. All being an angel got me was a single hearing."

"Hearing?"

"At the end of the world."

"What?"

"Oh right. I only ever talked to Cindy about this stuff. I forget that other people don't know about it."

"What happened?"

This time, he did speak quietly.

"Six years after I arrived on Earth, my brothers and sisters sought to destroy the world."

"The Seraphim? Why? I thought they were the good guys."

"Because they wear white and glow like fucking jewellery? Real good guys don't sacrifice worlds, Kat. And they don't look like they're from a choir. Real saints look like scum, and real scum look like saints. The Seraphim were so obsessed with their need for order, that they would destroy an entire world because it may or may not have allowed the demons of Raz'ed entry to the In Between."

"Earth…was almost destroyed? What stopped it?"

"I like to think that I did. But it was more Azrael."

"The angel of death?"

"Not in fact. She is the daughter of the Emperor of Raz'ed. A demon. But there is little difference between many demons and angels. We are of the same essence. And while my brothers and sisters may think themselves on the light-side of the spectrum, I believe they have just as much darkness in their hearts as the infernal legions. No being should have as much power as we can have. And no matter the best of intentions, absolute power corrupts absolutely."

"What did Azrael do?"

Conrad looked at me, intensely.

"She sacrificed herself. Her freedom. Her power. Everything. To keep the gate shut. To make it that the Seraphim wouldn't need to destroy Earth. And she left me…"

The waitress arrived to ask for our order. Conrad didn't speak, so I ordered for him. Sausages and mash. They made it well here. Conrad didn't continue after the waitress left.

"What happened afterwards?" I finally pressed. "Why are you no longer an angel?"

"I technically still am. But without my powers. I could probably show off my wings but wouldn't be able to use them. And my purification magic is dead. I would need to use a weyline if I was to get back in the game. But…"

He looked down at his untouched glass.

"I don't feel up to it anymore, Kat. I'm tired. Too tired. And I need a rest."

He looked at me, with a sadness that I'd never thought possible on his face.

"I'm sorry, Kat. Sorry that I have to abandon you. That I couldn't see you off until the end. And that my final mission for you caused…this. I told you once that you're a good hunter. I was wrong. You're the best."

"Pfft. Far from it."

"Don't call an old man a liar."

"You don't look a day over forty."

"I'm eight thousand years old, give or take. And that is much too long to be…anything. And most of that time, I did not feel alive. Until now. These past forty years on your…our planet…have been the greatest years of my eternity. Despite all the pain. Despite the risk that I may lose it all."

"Lose it?"

He shook his head. "No. It won't happen. You won't let it happen."

"Let what happen?"

He smiled, knowingly. "You will find out. When it matters. If it matters."

I was about to argue when the waitress, irritatingly dutiful, asked if she could refill my ale. I declined.

"While searching the Digby connection," he said, not letting me continue the previous topic (sly devil!). "I discovered something interesting."

"That he was a member of the Conclave?"

"How did you know that?"

I pointed at Candace's eye.

"She worked for them?" he asked.

"Yes. While biding her time. Then she flipped and destroyed a lot of their work. She's the one who led me to Jeremiah. All that time ago."

"She's a sly one."

"She's a child."

"So are you."

That silenced me. Conrad continued.

"Digby was a member of this elusive secret society that is known in the shadows and dark web as The Conclave. The full name, I have found, being the Conclave of the 6th Convent. I don't know what it means. What I did find out was that the Conclave was in conflict with our own local legend, Adam Dawi. The chairperson of Hope City who signed the treaty with the ogres, took back 1/3rd of the Three Point Line and dodged 4 out of 5 assassination attempts. The fifth, I am sure, was the work of the Conclave."

"I thought Dawi was killed by a disgruntled staffer."

"A disgruntled staffer, who whispers in Cindy's circles say, was under the effect of a mindwarp."

"Why isn't this public knowledge?"

"The same reason that council and police corruption is seldom reported on. Nobody cares and the people who do care don't want anybody to care. Succinctly, the Conclave owns the media."

"Typical. A secret society owns the media."

"Very typical. But that's how it remains secret. It sinks its claws into many things, to keep mouths shut and its coffers full."

"I find it hard to believe," I said. "A conspiracy this large would have been discovered. Too many cooks spoil the broth and this sounds like a horde of cooks. Someone would have betrayed them. Squealed. Gotten drunk."

"Well, we know. So, they aren't impervious. But I suspect there's some magic at play. Lawmancy, probably. Holding their tongues. Your departed boyfriend may have known more."

I averted my gaze.

"Sorry," Conrad said. "Thoughtless of me."

Our food arrived and we ate. After we were done, we continued speaking properly.

"The Conclave, I suspect, does not only have its hooks in the media and Council. I trust your rogue expedition into

Whiteshield last year was fruitful and you discovered what I did."

"Whiteshield owns MonsterSlayer? Yep."

"And the Conclave, I strongly believe, owns Whiteshield."

"Great! The largest paramilitary in Southern Africa is owned by the gang which tried to help my old priest destroy the world."

"It's not that simple, I suspect. The Conclave aren't madmen, like the people they use. At least, I don't think so. Groups like this, no matter how evil they may appear, tend not to contain the overly selfish or psychotic. If it has survived for this long, it means there is a degree of altruism in its ranks. People willing to sacrifice their own betterment for a shot at the success of their larger goal."

"And what is their larger goal?"

"I don't know. But even if it is charitable, I don't presume it is something we'll like."

I nodded my agreement but then frowned.

"So, a secret organisation has got it in for me, but can't get an arrest warrant to stick, so is pettily trying to starve me out. What am I? A medieval fortress?"

Conrad snorted, amused. "Regardless of your architectural integrity, we need to sort this out. Get you back on the hunt."

"Brett is going to try and get me a job at Drakenbane."

Conrad scowled. I laughed.

"Beats unemployment."

"They aren't your style, Kat. Too military. You don't have a personality in there. You'll just be a cog in their machine."

"Maybe for a bit. But we know people in that machine. There are decent people there. And I can do good from there. Until I find a way to get around this Conclave and get my freelancing license back."

Conrad nodded just as the busybody waitress came over with the bill. He paid.

"Thanks, Conrad. For the meal. For the info. For…everything."

"I failed you, Kat. I tried to make sure you'd be set after my retirement. Now all I can do is buy you a small meal."

"It's not your fault that I like making enemies."

We stood to say our goodbyes.

"I'll still help you. If I can. I don't have an agent license anymore, but I'll still try to help. To reinstate your license, to investigate this Conclave, to fight them if necessary."

I ambushed him with a hug. He was shocked, for a second, but then put his hands on my back and hugged me in return.

"That's all I ask for, Conrad. And I still say thank you. You helped me enter this life. Good for me or not, it's the life I wanted. And I'll make sure I get back to it."

I released him and we made our way to the exit.

"There is something you can help me with…"

"Anything…within reason!"

"My friend. Trudie. The goth girl that didn't like you."

"What about her?"

"She's disappeared. Told her parents that she's gone to visit family in America, but Pranish suspects she's still in Hope City."

He nodded. "I'll find her."

"Thanks, Conrad."

I smiled, and then made my way home.

Chapter 5. Drakenbane

"Stop fidgeting!" Treth scolded me, as we sat idle in a well-lit corporate waiting room that managed to feel not only soulless, but drab. The waiting room was large, but possessed seating for only around four people, forcing them to sit on those uncomfortable metal chairs that should never be present in any place which wishes to make its guests feel welcome.

I didn't know I had been fidgeting until Treth had rudely interrupted it. I had been tapping the scales on my flaming coat. Every time I lifted my finger, the coat let out a small column of flames where I had poked it.

I didn't respond to Treth but, feeling self-conscious, I leant back and put my hands in my pants pockets. I could probably have spoken to my ghostly companion without any problems. I was alone in the room, without even the courtesy of royalty-free waiting room music. But I didn't really feel like talking to him. We were still fighting. And besides, walls have ears. Knowing these corporates, they were probably watching me right now. Judging me. Seeing if I was agency material. But what even was agency material? I saw how the hunters acted on the job, and it wasn't so different from how I acted. But, in the confines of these halls, in Old Town skyscrapers, my friends took on a new personality. They became robots. Busani, Brett and Guy's friend, saw me and, instead of his usual wide smile, he only nodded. Sternly. To be fair on Drakenbane, this reaction may have been due to the fact that last time I saw Busani, it had been with Whiteshield shooting at us. He may be trying to deny our relationship to avoid suspicion. Or…he resented me.

I really hoped it wasn't the latter.

I sat upright as the door in front of me opened. Brett was still talking to someone behind him as he exited.

"And you've been saying for a while we need to move in on Puretide's territory…"

"Yes, yes, Agent Callahan. But it's her turn to be interviewed. I'm sure she appreciates your testimony," replied a stern looking woman wearing glasses and a tight bun. She was wearing a beige business dress with a Drakenbane pin on her lapel.

"Ms Drummond? I'll meet with you now."

Brett beamed at me as I stood and followed the unsmiling lady into her office. He gave me a double thumbs up as the door closed behind me.

"Please, take a seat."

I thanked her and sat down in a comfortable leather chair (with armrests!) facing a larger variant of the same chair on the other side. A mahogany desk divided us. Behind her chair was Hope City's Old Town. In particular, an UhuruTech billboard, a five-star hotel and a glimpse of the ocean. Drakenbane HQ was built on prime real estate. Perhaps I should stop fretting about the loss of my independence. They were prestigious. I could go places with them.

"Ms Drummond."

She woke me from my reverie.

"Yes?"

"I am Recruitment Manager Bertha DeKoop. I am responsible for finding, assessing, interviewing and, finally, recruiting new operators and agents for the Drakenbane Monster Hunting Agency. For this interview, you may call me Bertha."

"Thank you, Bertha. You can call me Kat."

"Ms Drummond," she called me, still. "Are you nervous for this interview?"

Was I? What an odd question.

"As nervous as is natural, I suppose," I replied.

She nodded. I'm not sure if understandingly or sceptically.

"Your...colleague, Agent Callahan, speaks highly of you."

"I hope not too highly. He can tell big mermaid stories."

"Humble?"

I smiled, faintly.

"Humility is not an automatic virtue."

My smile faded.

"Agent Callahan reports that you have worked with Drakenbane agents before. First, during the impromptu purging of the University of Cape Town Campus last year. Is this true? Can you provide some details?"

I nodded. "It is true. I was a student on campus during the zombie attack. I met up with Brett...Agent Callahan, Agent Mgebe and Auxiliary-Agent Giles. We worked together to bring down the necromancer responsible."

"Are you still a student?"

"No."

"You were in second year during the purge. Did you finish your degree early?"

"I decided that a tertiary education of that kind was not appropriate for my desired vocation."

She nodded and wrote something down. I hope something positive, but I doubted it.

"It says here that you faced a magistrate for your killing of the necromancer."

"It was ruled that I acted in self-defence."

She almost snorted.

"Convenient, that."

She looked up and must have seen my worry. She laughed.

"Don't worry. We understand. If an agent here doesn't have to face a magistrate within a year of recruitment, they aren't doing their job properly."

I almost sighed with relief.

"Agent Callahan reported that you worked in tandem with Drakenbane, Puretide and freelance hunters during the Necrolord Operations last year. I fear that I could not find records of your involvement, however."

I clenched my fist under the desk. Fucking James Montague. Screwing me from the grave.

"Public bureaucracy," I replied.

She nodded, understandingly. I couldn't help but start to like her. And began to relax.

"Both Agent Mgebe and Agent Callahan have written testimonials. So has Auxiliary-Agent Giles, yet I regret that she is no longer with the agency as her term has run out and she has returned to Heiliges Licht. But, her opinion is regarded highly. In fact, more highly than that of our permanent agents."

I'd have to thank her later for that! It seemed I was always thanking Cindy these days.

"Ms Giles states that you are an effective operator, with a profound knowledge of the undead, vampires and demons."

The latter, I wasn't so sure about. Had I even killed any demons? I don't think so. But I wasn't going to contradict Cindy! She was the expert, after all.

"How would you describe your expertise, Ms Drummond?"

"I stab things."

She raised her eyebrow. "That's all?"

"I know where to stab them," I added, grinning. My grin wilted as she didn't laugh and noted something down.

"I also use a handgun," I answered, serious now. "An enchanted piece that can be used to fight demons and spirits."

"Drakenbane does not often deal with demons and spirits."

"But they do come up. And when they do, you need an effective operator to deal with them."

She considered my words, then noted them down.

"The coat?" she asked, simply.

I turned in my chair so she could get a look. It flared, slightly.

"A salamander coat. I killed it last year. It has grown a liking for me since then. And it has saved my skin enough times that I've grown a liking for it."

"Salamanders are more Drakenbane's bread and butter, to use the colloquialism. But, we have a building full of drake hunters. Let us cut to the chase. Drakenbane is considering employing you to begin its diversification into undead hunting."

If I was Duer, I would have glowed. If Drakenbane was hunting zoms, then they would definitely hire me! And I'd get to kill what I wanted to kill.

"The spate of undead attacks and the Necrolord Operation last year revealed that, despite our competitor, Puretide's, best efforts, undead hunting is still an open market. We seek to change that by recruiting hunters like yourself to stem the tide. And, because our data doesn't show that the tide can be stemmed, we believe this is a sustainable market. What do you think of this notion, Ms Drummond?"

That caught me by surprise. I considered her words, quickly.

"The undead are caused by two factors. Rift-surges, which are arbitrary, albeit rare. And necromancers. Necromancy is a trained art, so the supply of undead can be replenished as long as there are necromancers reanimating them."

"So, is this business strategy sound?"

I had never really thought about that. I just killed them because…

"While drakes are bigger money," I said. "Undead are much less rewarding per a head. But there is a distinct advantage with undead hunting. It's cheap. You just need something sharp or heavy."

"And this is why you did it?"

That felt like an insult. I chose not to treat it as such.

"I hunt them because they are a threat that needs to be culled. But, also yes. Hunting bigger game requires a bigger investment. One that a freelancer cannot make."

"So, undead hunting appeals more to freelancers."

I nodded. "And Puretide won't even deal with small undead attacks, so freelancers find a lot of work that the agencies won't take."

"And what is your assessment of this? Should Drakenbane, for instance, take an interest in smaller cases?"

"A monster is a monster. And if it pays, it pays. Small cash mounts up. And while I have not done the maths, I'm a swordswoman after all, I'm sure you'll find that there are financial benefits to cheap hunts. With the savings on ammunition and large calibre rounds, you may find that hunting zombies makes more profits than hunting dragons."

"Interesting, Ms Drummond. And something we shall consider. Before I proceed with more questions, are there any you have about Drakenbane?"

Brett and Guy had prepared me for this.

"No, thank you."

She nodded, satisfied.

"Last question. A scenario: You are running a solo mission against a lich. A high value target in your specialty. Assume for this scenario that you have the capacity to eliminate this lich, as Agent Callahan assures me that you do. But, during the operation, you are faced with a choice. The lich is getting away, but can be pursued, but in the centre of his ritual room are two non-clients, a middle-aged woman and a young boy. You recognise the ritual to be a draining ritual, slowly stealing their souls. They will die within a minute if not freed. What do you do?"

"I save them," I answered, without hesitation.

She raised an eyebrow. "The lich will get away."

"I will still save them."

"They cannot afford to pay you or the agency."

"I save them," I repeated. "It is the right thing to do. And even if they cannot pay me, they will know that I saved them. And others will know I did the right thing. People will hire me again because they know I put human life before profit. Which leads to profit in the long-term."

"But what if, hypothetically, they will not and cannot know that you saved them."

"I will still save them," I insisted. "And simply because it is the right thing to do."

She wrote down some notes in silence, and then stood. She offered her hand.

"This has been an interesting interview, Ms Drummond. I will contact you within a few days."

"Do you not make the final decision?"

"There is protocol, Ms Drummond. I will contact you. Thank you."

I turned at her indication and exited. Brett was waiting for me outside.

"How did it go?" he asked, initially buzzing, but his expression sombre at my look of excitement.

"Most of it was fine," I said quietly. Brett indicated for us to take the elevator down, out of earshot of the recruitment manager.

"But the last question…" I continued. "I don't think she liked my answer."

"Did you save them or go for the contract?"

I looked at him questioningly.

"We all get the same last question. I gave the right answer."

"Which was?"

"I went for the contract."

"Brett!"

He raised his hands defensively.

"Trust me! It wasn't about the money. The contract in mine was a vampire."

I understood. I didn't like it, but I understood. Brett, especially when he would have joined up, despised vampires above all. I could understand him ignoring everything else to go for the kill.

"Kat, what did you answer?"

"That I'd save them."

He shook his head.

"Should have lied."

"Why?"

"This is a monster hunting agency. Not a rescue agency."

"But our clients are humans…sometimes otherworlders."

"And they pay us to kill things. Not to save lives. Especially unpaying lives."

"You've saved me. You saved Trudie."

"And fat pay check it got me."

He grinned and I elbowed him in the ribs.

"Still, Kat. It wouldn't have hurt for you to lie. How did the rest of it go?"

"Well, I think well. Your testimony must have pre-answered most of her questions."

He looked smug.

"If it's a thanks you want, then you can wait until I have the job."

We stopped at a floor and the doors opened to no one. We waited and they closed, and we continued our descent in silence.

"But…" I whispered, my cheeks heating up. "Thanks."

Chapter 6. Conspiracy

Days passed and I accepted an invitation to eat at the Davison's (with Pranish absent), Cindy's and once with Miriam LeBlanc, who gave me a book on vampire lore.

"Just because you've realised the futility of academia doesn't mean you can't continue learning," she said. I was very relieved to find out she actually supported my decision to drop-out. She said she was giving herself another year and then quitting UCT herself. Academia was toxic, she argued. They didn't care about the truth. Only spamming journals and being collectively smug.

While I wouldn't accept Brett's money, for dignity and other reasons, I was more than willing to eat for free. I'm only human!

During this time, I also had a slight breakthrough with Treth. He expressed an interest in learning how to hunt lesser drakes and we used Miriam's library pass to get into the UCT library and read up on the creatures. Even though we were still not as relaxed with each other as we once were, I felt that this was like old times. Researching monsters, together, surrounded by dust and tomes. In a way, it was our peace treaty, and it meant that we could be friends again, once we got over our issues.

I was at home on the fifth day following my Drakenbane interview when I heard a knock on the door.

"Don't cheat," I told Duer. We were playing *Go Fish*. I knew he was going to cheat, so I hoped that whoever was at the door had a good excuse.

I answered the door to Guy. He looked…pissed. Like, really angry. As bad as when I saw him kill vampires, even. And behind him was Brett, facing away. His arms crossed. I couldn't see his expression, but I knew that he was seething.

"What happened?" I immediately asked, unable to hide the fear in my voice.

Guy barged in, giving me barely enough time to back away so he could pass through.

"What happened?!" I repeated.

Brett followed. He avoided my eyes. Guy was pacing. Duer must've felt the tension was a bit too much for him and had disappeared inside his birdhouse.

I was about to repeat the question, when Guy started.

"Drakenbane declined your application."

He said, simply and angrily. But his anger was about something else.

"Fuck, well. Back to the drawing board." I tried to smile but failed. Just my fucking luck. Was it because of my jokes? Or because I insisted that I save before kill?

"It's more than that." Guy pointed accusingly at Brett.

"This moron, in his infinite wisdom, staged a one-man protest in Drakenbane HQ, accusing them of corruption and collusion with corrupt cops and secret societies."

I looked at Brett with dismay.

"You didn't!"

Guy nodded, irritably. "He fucking did. And, understandably, they fired him."

"Brett…I'm sorry."

"Don't be," Guy interjected. "Because then they fired me."

"What?!"

"I said the same thing. I was out getting coffee and donuts for the floor with Busani when I see this guy storming out of HR. Then I get called in!"

"Did…did they say why?"

"The usual corporate claptrap. That they are cutting costs. And that they are over-capacity."

"They were short twenty men last week," Brett mumbled.

"Thanks, Captain Obvious! Or should that be Civilian Obvious, now?"

Brett made a threatening motion towards his friend and I stepped in his way, putting my hand on his chest and holding up another anticipating Guy. But even if his words were harsh, Guy could still keep a cool head. He didn't make a move.

"Kat…we're out of a job. No license. No pay check," Guy said. He didn't sound angry. It was…more pleading.

"Welcome to the club," I said, despairingly. I hated the tone in my voice.

The room fell silent. I even felt the tension from Duer.

What were we going to do?

"I…I'm sorry. This is my fault."

"It's not…" Brett started. I squeezed the fabric on his shirt to quieten him.

"No. I shouldn't have let you stick your necks out for me. I've got too many enemies and now I've made them yours."

I shook my head and let go of Brett's shirt. He looked calm now. Guy leant up against the wall. He was staring blankly into space.

"I should've just gone back to data-entry."

"At least you can," Guy said. "All Brett and I have ever known is killing."

"Data-entry isn't exactly a job that requires much work experience. I could try to get you…"

"No thanks. At least, not yet." Brett tried to smile. Failed.

"We'll find something, Kat," Guy said, but he sounded resigned. "MonsterSlayer may accept our application for a license and then we can slay the way you did. Perhaps we'll be even better at it."

"And then we can add you to the team," Brett added. "We act as the front and you get part of the pay."

"Let's not divide up the loot before there's any loot," Guy said, sounding irritated.

"I hope it works out, guys. I really do. And if you accept it or not, I'm sorry. For everything and more. And I'll make this right."

Chapter 7. Eviction

When it rains, it storms. MonsterSlayer denied Brett and Guy's license application. Like me, they were not allowed to legally hunt monsters under Hope City's laws. They didn't know what to do, except live off their savings and start selling off their vast collection of legal and not-so-legal weapons. Guy didn't speak to me. Only Brett did. And he visited me almost every day. I didn't mind. Far from it. He was bored. I was bored. Duer got tired of the company. He was introverted by nature. On the third day of Brett coming to visit, just to pore over Miriam's book in silence while I played games on my phone, Duer yelled (or more accurately: squeaked):

"When will ye all get outta me space?!"

I felt for my pixie, despite his rudeness. Our arrangement had previously worked because I was so rarely home. Pixies deplored constant company. Especially, non-fae company. Unfortunately, Brett and I were very much unfae-like, and Duer was taking strain.

Brett and I obliged my pixie roommate as we went to visit Cindy and my cat, who I like to think misses me, but seemed overly comfortable in Cindy's larger home. She also had a yard, which he appreciated. I was happy for him. Even if it meant he preferred someone else to me. You know what they say? You love someone, you let them go.

(Fucking cat.)

Brett walked me home from Cindy's as it approached evening. It was still summer, and the sun took a while to go down. Brett treated me to a burger and chips. Very healthy. I reminded him that we couldn't rely on our jobs to keep us in shape anymore. He pretended to ignore me, but I saw that it stung. And regretted saying it.

There was a lot of activity around my apartment when we got back. Men were removing Mrs Ndlovu's "Beware of the Wraith" signs and there was a man overseeing what looked to be construction workers. I thought nothing of it until I saw a man carrying Duer's birdhouse. With him still in it.

"What are you doing with my pixie?!"

I ran towards the worker manhandling my pixie, with the thought to knock him to the ground. A young man bearing a striking resemblance to my landlady stepped in my way and I skidded to a halt.

"Ms Drummond? Yes. Probably. You are behind on rent."

"Excuse me! Who are you?"

"I am Patrice Ndlovu. I am the new owner."

"Where is Mrs Ndlovu?"

"My…beloved…mother has passed away. The pain of losing my father in December was too much and now she is with the gods."

"My…my condolences."

"Yes, quite." He eyed me up and down, his gaze resting on my flaming coat.

"My mother noted down in her ledger that you were behind on rent, but was allowing you to stay despite this, due to the goodness of her heart and that you were a trusted tenant. Moreover, she was undercharging you for a premium apartment for years."

"Mrs Ndlovu, your mother, knew that I paid when I could. And I always did…"

"Except when you didn't." He sighed and crossed his arms. "My mother was a kind woman. But I risk the ancestor's wrath when I say that she was wrong many times. And I am certain she was wrong to trust you."

I opened my mouth to argue and he raised a finger.

"You were exploiting my poor mother. And I won't let you exploit me. I have already moved your possessions to the yard. Please dispose of them within the hour or I will report you to the police for illegal dumping."

I saw my possessions, as few as there now were, piled in the front lawn. My books, my notes, my laptop, kettle, blankets, pillows, Brett's swords. Even Voidshot, discarded haphazardly next to Duer's birdhouse, which he stood on disgruntled as a wet cat.

"Where's the fridge?"

"It belongs to the apartment."

"I bought it myself," I hissed.

"With money owed to my mother."

"She bought it herself," Brett said. The menace in his voice caused Patrice to back away.

"She's a thief, whoever you are. She should be thankful that I'm letting her keep anything!"

Brett's hand drifted to his waistband. My heart skipped a beat and I reached for his hand, grasping it to prevent him from drawing his gun. He looked at my hand in his and seemed to forget all about his potential homicide.

"Please," I pleaded, trying to be diplomatic. You know I've been losing a lot when I try this approach. "I have nowhere to stay. You saw the room. I don't even have any food."

"You want charity?"

He laughed.

"Did your people give mine charity forty years ago? Fifty? A hundred? No. You dominated us."

"And now you own three quarters of what was once a country," Brett remarked.

"And it will be four quarters!" Patrice spat, pointing accusingly at Brett. He turned his back on us.

"Remove your belongings before my patience wears even thinner."

He walked to his construction crew. I didn't try to pursue. I knew I was in the wrong. And it wasn't about fairness. I had, in a way, exploited Mrs Ndlovu's kindness. But now…

I knelt next to the pile of everything I owned and examined my pixie.

"Did they hurt you?"

"They wouldn't dare!"

I smiled, weakly. "I'm glad."

I felt tears well up, but Brett's presence behind me stopped me. He put his hand on my back.

"I'll get the van."

"Where will I stay?" I felt the question was rhetorical. More resignation than anything else.

"You…you can stay with me."

I looked at him. My heart beat fast. And I couldn't understand why. He looked at me so earnestly, and sadly. He wanted this. But, how could I? After what I'd done to him and Guy. He may have forgiven me, but Guy was still irritable. But it was more than that…

"I…I don't think I can."

"You can! Guy will be fine with it. I'll make sure he's fine with it. And we can convert the armoury into a room. It's not like we need as many weapons anymore…"

"Brett!" I stopped him.

He shushed, but still buzzed like a puppy waiting for a ball to be thrown.

"I don't think it's appropriate," I said. It's all I felt I could say.

"Not appropriate?" he looked broken.

"Why not move in with Cindy?" Duer offered. "The lass has plenty o' room. And the demon-feline misses me."

"Why is it inappropriate?" Brett pressed.

"It just is!"

"You were fine living with that other guy…" he mumbled.

My cheeks reddened, and not with embarrassment. I felt a rage come over me.

"I loved that *guy*. And he's now dead. I don't want to live with you, Brett!"

I expected an outburst. Some yelling back. I hoped for him to yell back. He didn't. He looked hurt. Very hurt. He turned his back on me.

"I'll get the van," he said, again. And walked off.

I took a while to gather my things. At least, wherever I ended up, I didn't have much left to move.

Chapter 8. Ghosts

Cindy was still not home when we parked outside her house. I phoned her and told her what had happened. Before I had finished, she immediately offered me her spare room. I thanked her profusely. We had spare keys to get in, in case of emergencies. Unloading my meagre possessions didn't take long.

I thanked Brett after moving my stuff. He didn't respond. I felt worry rise and then anger. He got into his van and drove away before I could yell at him or apologise. But I didn't feel like I needed to apologise! It's my right to not move in with him. And what he said about Colin, as if I owed him…

I felt a seething rage well up inside of me. But without even a punching bag, the anger turned to frustration. Even my cat curling his way around my legs couldn't calm me. I ran to the bathroom, shut the door behind me. And screamed. I felt Candace watch me, for a second, and then return to her own pain. I fell to my knees, and when my voice became too hoarse, I put my head under the cold tap, and put it on full blast. Soaked, I looked at myself in the mirror. Two different coloured eyes. Still scarred. A missing streak of hair where a wraith had scalped me. My eyes, both Candace's and mine, were puffy. I wanted to sleep. But I didn't want to sleep. I was tired, but I wanted to kill something.

"We've been through worse, Kat," Treth said, and it wasn't his recent tone of derision. It was sincere. Concerned.

"What do I fucking do, Treth?"

"What we always do. We find a way."

"But what is the way?"

He couldn't reply. I sat on the cold tile floor and held my head in my hands.

"Kat, how long have we been together?"

I didn't answer immediately. But then mumbled, "Three years."

"So short? Yet, it feels like we've been together a lifetime."

"Getting sentimental on me, Treth?" I tried to laugh. I only managed to gather a snort.

"Kat, you've changed. In all these years. Not just physically. You've gotten better. Better at fighting. Better at seeing what's right and wrong. Better at living this life."

"You don't seem to think that all the time."

"I'm not old, Kat. I think you know that. And, at a time, we were equals. But not anymore. While you have been aging, I have stayed the same. And the longer we stay tethered, the more I fear that I won't be able to mature. To truly mature. Everything I learn, I learn through you. And that means…I can't be my own man, Kat. And that is why I think your relationship with the Necro…with Candace frustrated me so much. It's because it was a decision I wouldn't have made. And it reminded me that I couldn't make decisions anymore."

I stared at the tiles, small puddles forming from my wet hair.

"I miss my body, Kat. And I miss being my own person. And I know this is unfair for me to say to you. Because I'm a parasite who resents its host. But…"

"I love you, Treth," I said, and felt his shock. "And we're in this together. And we may disagree. And we may get tired of each other. But I accepted long ago that this was our lot."

I stood up, suddenly and made my way to where I had left my possessions. I loaded my two remaining rounds into Voidshot's stripper-clip. Brett had left his swords. I attached my sword-belt. Treth didn't ask what I was doing. I think he knew. My coat ignited. It knew too.

"Am I going to get some peace, at last?" Duer asked.

"Shut up, Duer."

He stuck his tongue out at me and flew to Cindy's potplant, which he started singing to.

I scribbled a note for Cindy and left it on the coffee table. I locked the front door behind me.

I took a deep breath. It was going to be a long night.

Chapter 9. Where I belong

The zombie was missing an arm. But that didn't slow it down. Or discourage it one little bit. It let out spittle as it dove towards me. I dodged just at the last second, letting it collide with a brick wall. Its skull cracked. I cut its head off just to make sure.

"Right," Treth called.

I slashed right, and spun, cutting into a zombie and then pulling it into another. Its head was cut loose, and its collapsed torso tripped up its comrades. Blackened blood sprayed like gel, hissing as it hit my coat.

More walking corpses shambled into view at the end of the slum alleyway. They saw me and charged. They were fast. Not like in the old films. When a zombie had proper motivation, they could sprint with the best.

"They just keep coming, don't they?" I grunted.

"Yeah. Great, isn't it?"

I realised I was grinning.

I ducked low. The first zombie's momentum carried it over my back. My coat singed it and the smell of burnt flesh replaced the smell of rot. The smell I had gotten so used to.

In my own way, I loved it. Because it smelled like the place I belonged.

"Charge forward."

I did so, without hesitation. The zombie that had barrelled over me fell to the ground. Its eyes burnt and bubbling. I used my two swords to skewer the zombie in front of me. Twisted the hilts and pulled outwards. The zombie split like a melon, its sides peeling and falling to the ground. A memory of a past self would have vomited. I did not. With intense satisfaction, I pulled back my blades and let the rest of the zombie's body fall.

Growls behind me warned me before Treth did. I blindly slashed behind me, pirouetting and beheading a zombie. My pirouette ended as my blade hit a wall with a clunk. A zombie leapt forward, and I turned, letting my coat crisp it as I skewered an additional two zombies at once.

The tide stopped and I panted, heavily. But I was laughing. I hadn't felt this good in a long time.

"I needed this," I said.

"Me too."

"I'm sorry for…yeah."

"It's fine. I won't lie and say I understand what you feel for Candace, but it's not my business."

A zombie charged down the alley. I side stepped and it ran clean into my blade. Its headless body ran a few more metres before collapsing.

"I must say, however, I prefer killing zombies to fighting alongside them," Treth added.

"Me too."

I proceeded to another alley, where zombies were bashing on windows and peoples' doors. It was a practical epidemic! Only reason nobody cared was that it was in the slums. And that meant I didn't need a license to deal with it. It also meant I wasn't getting paid. But at this moment, I didn't care about that.

I took the head off the closest zombie to me.

"What do you think…" Dodged and beheaded another. "…of Brett's offer?"

"I preferred Colin."

"Colin is dead."

Treth sighed. "Colin would have dealt non-violently with Patrice. Used the law. May have even gotten you your fridge back."

"What would you have done?"

I felt him grin. "I would have cut his head off."

My laugh attracted the attention of two zombies, who charged me. I dispatched them. These weren't skilled walking corpses. Probably didn't even have a necromancer anymore. Knowing my luck, they were probably the remnants of Candace's army.

"You know why I don't think you like Brett?"

"Why?" Treth asked. "Behind you."

I cut low and brought the zombie to its knees. Its skull split like a coconut as its head impacted on the floor.

"You're like him."

"Pfft."

"No, really. Besides his clownishness, there's something about both of you. An earnestness. An honour. And…" I frowned, even as I killed the last zombie in the alley. "There's a deep pain."

"We're all in pain. Nothing special."

"You told me once…"

I was cut off by a scream. A child.

I ran towards the sound, all previous thoughts gone.

Zombies packed the alley and I slashed them when I couldn't dodge past. The screams continued, followed by shouting and banging.

A veritable horde were grasping towards the rooftop of a shanty. They were clambering over each other, attempting to use one another as an undead ladder to get to a woman and two children.

There were a lot of zombies. Too many. Even for me.

The woman was kicking at the zombies. One grabbed her foot and tore off her shoe.

I knew what Treth would do. I did the same.

I charged the zombies. A few turned to face me. I slashed their throats. Shallow wounds. Noncommittal. They'd live.

I ducked at the edge of the mosh-pit and slashed the ankles of the back row. They fell and I leapt, using them as steps. I trudged on the shoulders of surprised zombies, cutting their curious hands. I found firm footing on the edge of the shanty's roof and slashed wide, pushing back the rising tide.

The woman looked at me, confused and desperate.

"Get to that roof," I said, pointing at the neighbouring house. She hesitated. I yelled. "Get to the roof!"

She stood up and carried her smaller child while leading the older one by the hand. A zombie made it up to the roof. I stuck my one blade into its back and, as it clawed at my boots, I cut off its head.

The woman was struggling to lift both her children to the next roof, while the zombies didn't relent. They couldn't relent. It was in the name, after all. The relentless, never ceasing, never desisting, never resting…dead.

"They need help," Treth stated, a hint of anxiety in his voice. But also…confidence. He believed I could do it.

A zombie clambered up onto my rooftop. I stuck both my swords into its head and dragged it closer in, using it as a make-shift sheath. It clawed impotently as its head was pinned to the roof.

I grabbed the older child and lifted her up to the higher rooftop. The woman passed the toddler to his sister and then clambered up herself. A zombie, who had used its comrade to climb up to our perch, charged me. I kicked it back, retrieved my swords, and then swiftly cut its head off with both blades in unison. The woman offered me a hand. I sheathed one sword and accepted it. She helped lift me up.

"We can't keep climbing," Treth said.

"But we can make this someone else's problem," I replied, out-loud. To the woman's bemusement.

I spoke to her. "Follow me."

I ran across the higher rooftop. The zombies were struggling to get the footing to get this high, but it was only a matter of time.

The woman huffed as she ran. Her daughter looked much calmer. In a way, I was proud of her. Even if I didn't know her.

A gap ended the rooftop. On the other side was a concrete structure, with a doorway on the roof. Behind us, the zombies had managed to scale the structure to our level.

"We have to jump!" I called.

The woman backed away, shaking her head. The zombies' feet were a storm on the metal roof. She looked back at them, and at me.

"You go first. And I'll pass him to you."

She looked at her daughter. She nodded. I accepted the toddler. The zombies were getting closer.

The woman made the jump.

"You go," I said to the girl. She nodded again and made a running jump. Her mom caught her.

The thuds were too loud. They were almost on us.

I reached out the toddler. He was crying. His arms were outstretched to his mom. She leant as close as she could to him. Her daughter held onto her clothes, pulling with all her might. I strained and strained. I could hear the zombies roar.

She managed to take him from me.

"Dodge!" Treth yelled.

I did so, and the zombie passed centimetres from the toddler, falling to the floor below. But its arm caught the child and the woman let go. She screamed, as I dove down.

The light of my coat illuminated the alleyway as I descended. As I engulfed the weeping boy in my arms and held him close. Willing him to be okay. To survive. No matter what else happened.

My coat blazed.

And I hit something crunchy that broke my fall. Other zombies landed near us, like rain. The boy was still in my arms, sniffling, but no longer crying.

"Door," Treth called, drawing my attention to the wall of the alley.

I saw the door and shoved it open with my shoulder. I used a free hand to close it. I heard the muffled thuds of zombies hitting the floor. Some would die. Some would survive. I put the boy down on the floor and hefted a table in front of the door, despite the pain in my sides.

Everything went silent.

"Momma?"

I looked up. The boy was looking at his mother, who was holding her mouth in happy disbelief. She ran down the stairway and enfolded the boy in her arms. Her daughter joined her, and they cried together. In relief. In happiness.

I smiled.

"This is it, Treth," I said. "You told me once that I should not kill for hate. And I think you forgot that when you wanted Candace dead. And I know Brett doesn't know it, when he keeps killing vampires. But that isn't the real reason we should do this. Because as much as it felt good killing zombies…this feels better."

Treth and I watched together, half listening for the zombies to try and break in and half watching the family we had saved, as they held each other, weeping in joy for simply being alive.

Chapter 10. First Blood

Brett couldn't breathe. But he had never felt more alive. He still saw the grotesque visage of the vampiric monster in the church. Its killing of his comrades. The blood. All the blood. And the black tendrils, killing more effectively than bullets ever could. He had believed himself as good as dead. In a way, he looked forward to seeing his family again. Wherever they were. He stared death in the face. He did not accept it, but he expected it.

And then the sun shone. And the light replaced the dark.

The Corps.

The rotors of the chopper continued their melody, muffled now that Brett was inside. He did not recognise anyone in the chopper. They were older than he was. Grizzled. They did not wear the fatigues and uniform overalls of his company but were all personalised and kitted with armour and a multitude of expensive weaponry.

People did not last long in the Corps. But those who did…they seldom died. And a long bloody path of monsters was often left in their wake. Brett admired them. And feared them. But never believed he would become one of them. Yet, there was nothing else he wanted more.

The door to the cockpit opened, revealing a man with a black moustache, styled paper-thin. He was in his forties. Practically ancient. He had no scars. This was not a sign of privilege. Brett knew this man. And he knew that Finley was a warrior. So great a warrior that he had not been touched. For if the monsters he hunted were to touch him, he would become one of them.

"Callahan," Finley stated by way of greeting and accusation. Brett considered looking down at this blood-stained shoes and pants, but he knew what Finley wanted. He looked up, into Finley's eyes. The closest thing he, at least hoped, had for a friend nodded, and offered him a hand.

Brett accepted and squeezed Finley's hand as hard as he could, as Finley crushed his.

"You're alive," Finley said, simply.

"Yes, sir. Is the Third Company okay?"

"Okay, Callahan? It lost 55 of its 60 members. Terrible commanders, unflinching stupidity in the face of danger and blind fanaticism for a military turned cult led to destruction this day, my boy."

"So," Brett almost sighed, defeated. "The Third is gone."

"Never gone, Callahan. Look at me." Brett realised he had looked away. Finley held his chin. Not violently. Not tenderly. But in a way, fatherly.

"You are the Third, Brett," he said, not an ounce of doubt in his eyes or voice. "You are the Corps. And so long as you're living and slaying, the Third and the Corps will never die."

"Yes…yes, sir."

Finley released Brett's chin and took a seat opposite him. Brett noted that his heart was not pounding as much as before. He could breathe. And despite the memories he now had, the blood on his body, and the comrades he had lost, he felt – in a way – satisfied.

"Callahan," Finley said, speaking like a commander now rather than Brett's mentor. "Orientation was not completely truthful with you."

"Sir?"

"Get that out of your system. We'll soon be equals. Well, not exactly equals."

"Sir?" Brett dumbly repeated. Finley's lip twitched in amusement. Almost a smile. Almost.

"Upon surviving your orientation company, you are now to be assigned to a specialist squad befitting your skills and vendetta."

"Sir, I would like to be assigned to your squad."

He shook his head. "No, you don't, Callahan. We may both serve the same beloved Corps, and we may both come to kill the same monsters on every other day, we both have different reasons for hiding in the shadows to slay monsters. We love the Corps because it allows us to hate, my boy. And my hate is hairy and fanged, while yours is pale and fanged."

Brett's disappointment was very noticeable. Finley laughed.

"It's better this way. You wouldn't survive the Silver Squad. The Silver Brotherhood. Not because you don't have the guts. You more than do. But because you wouldn't have a reason to kill."

He shook his head to emphasise the point.

"No. You belong in Black Squad. The Defangers. You'll find your reason for living there. And you'll be able to sate your hatred."

"Sir, you're the one who saved me."

"You aren't saved, Brett. You're lost. I'm lost. And we are all lost. We are drowning in a sea of black mulch. Consumed by our loss, motivated by hate. We're too broken to stay afloat. Too angry to sink. The Corps is our only guiding light. The only thing that lets us come ashore. It lights up a path for us, Brett. But you know what's at the end of that path?"

Brett shook his head.

"Monsters," Finley whispered. "And through killing them, we make ourselves whole again."

***

Brett signed to his comrades. Three fingers. Two. One.

He turned and kicked down the aluminium plated door with a decisive blow. It flew on its hinges, smacking into the wall. Muzzle-flare lit up the darkness. Hisses responded to the bang.

Brett's shotgun-mounted flashlight illuminated an emaciated, blackening body, seething with rage. A ghoul. It lunged and Brett fired. Silver pellets shredded its cheeks and embedded in bone. It fell, but Brett didn't trust its ability to stay down.

He opened fire at a movement further into the darkness while advancing, his fellows behind him. The ghoul's chest heaved. He stomped on its head. His gut lurched at the sound. But his adrenaline and excitement prevented nausea.

"56, Groundhog, with me!" Brett's officer, nick-named Krieg, ordered. Brett was still just 56. He hadn't gotten a nickname yet.

Brett checked his angles, arcing his shotgun across the multiple doorways of this entry-hall. Clear. He moved to follow Krieg.

Gunshots sounded around the building. Not a silent operation. The Corps wanted to send a message, this time.

Goldfield land was not vampire land. No matter what international treaties might say. Bloodsuckers couldn't just hide behind some fancy lawyers and a jury of vamp-blood addicted thralls. If they wanted to live among humans in order to treat them like cattle, they had to fear the Corps.

Krieg held up his fist. Brett and Groundhog stopped. A woman screamed. Brett felt concern. For a second. The screaming stopped after a gunshot. If she was dead, it meant she was a vampire. She wasn't human. She was one of them.

He felt rage in his chest. Again. The same rage he felt every day. It fuelled him.

Krieg indicated with a wave of his hand to proceed.

In a dark blur, he was taken out from the side by a creature that didn't look vampire or human. Groundhog hesitated, and so did Brett. But Brett recovered first.

He charged the blur, even as blood spurted from his commander and the cacophony of extermination increased in volume. His shoulder met hard flesh and he was winded as he shoved the creature away. Groundhog recovered his senses and opened fire. A bullet drilled through the creature's chest, causing it to halt its blurring speed and grab onto its now smoking wound.

It looked like a cross between a small child, a bat and a rat. But all wrong. Its teeth were jagged and sharp, its claws as long as scissor blades and it had webbing underneath its arms. Its skin was grey and it had a thin layer of fur across its body. Brett pulled the trigger on his shotgun, just as he was jolted. The creature was fast and had hit his shotgun. Brett's heart beat fast as he fired again, not even aiming and hitting a doorframe. Something sharp bit into his arm and he cried out.

"Eyes!" Krieg half-shouted and half-rasped.

Brett closed his eyes and dove away from his officer, as a loud bang deafened him and left a ringing in his ears. Brett opened his eyes to the sight of the creature screaming, silently, rubbing its eyes to no avail, as it mindlessly clawed at its own face.

Brett took aim and fired, not hearing his own shot. The pellets eviscerated the creature's face and it fell from the force. Groundhog drew his silver-trim kukri and started chopping. No blood poured from the creature, but it stopped moving. Eventually.

Krieg, his face covered in welts and red cuts, pointed behind Brett and mouthed the words "Go." Brett nodded, even as his head still rung.

Corpses littered the passageways. Not Corpsmen. Not vampires. People. Emaciated. Drained. Some still breathed. But they were as good as dead. They would give up all their blood for just a little taste of vamp blood. Brett stepped over them carefully. His hearing started to return. The gunshots were rarer now. He heard Krieg yelling at Groundhog, who was applying first-aid to his butchered face.

Rapid tapping. Running.

Brett turned, lighting up the end of a room with his flashlight.

Nothing.

His heartbeat didn't slow down.

He hadn't seen a single humanoid vampire yet. Just ghouls and that creature. He hated them. But in the same way an arachnophobe hated spiders. It was a hatred for what they could do. What they represented. But he didn't hate them for what they were. The face of evil, he truly believed, was beautiful. Pale. With red eyes and succulent lips. They looked human. They pretended to be human. They came into your home. They befriended your parents. And then they chopped them up and escaped with your sister for dessert.

Leaving you alone.

All alone.

Crying. Wanting to die. Dying.

But if not for the light.

Drowning. If not for the light.

And the sound of choppers.

Hate saved him. Hate and the Corps.

And it was hate that kept him going in these dark halls, stenching of decay, faeces, iron and gunfire.

Brett almost jumped as he rounded a corner. The man around there almost jumped as well. But he wore the black of the Corps and saw that Brett wore the same. A corporal named Splinter came to the front.

"Krieg?" he asked.

"Wounded, sir. Groundhog's got him."

He nodded. "Fall in, 56. We're storming their last hold-out and need you on the frontline."

"Yessir."

The hold-out was behind a double door, already setup with breaching charges. Brett was in position to detonate the one closest to him and then open fire immediately. Even this far in the building, they heard sirens. The police would not stop them, but life would be easier for everyone if they ended this less than internationally legal raid soon.

The surviving Corpsmen fanned around the entrance to the hold-out, flanking the doorway. Krieg had recovered, just a bit, and was holding a .45 revolver. He levelled it at the door and gave the breachers the nod.

Brett clicked his detonator and it was time for his ears to ring again. Dust and debris filled the air and the muffled thuds of gunfire broke through the vibrations in his head after the explosion. He advanced through the soot and the manmade fog of destruction.

Pale faces. A lot of them. Red eyes. They looked human. They weren't human. Brett felt his heart ache. His breathing stopped. He levelled his shotgun and time froze.

It was easy to kill monsters that looked like monsters. But the real monsters looked human. And it was monsters that looked like these who had taken everything from him. Everything.

Time unfroze with a bang. And another. And another. The vampires were undefended. Some tried to lash out. Krieg burst in, his one eye covered with a bandage. He kicked a small vamp in the face, keeping it down. He pressed his foot into its chest. It clawed at his boot, trying to breathe even though it didn't need to. Krieg examined its face. Curiosity. Disgust. He fired and blood splattered. The vamp must've been new. It didn't stand a chance against the Corps.

Brett incapacitated vamps with a rain of pellets, allowing his comrades to eliminate them. Despite his adrenaline, he felt robotic. Unsatisfied. He kept shooting, but his rage didn't abate. And the despair niggling in the back of his mind was barely held back by his fury.

Vampires tried to escape through other doorways, windows and out the way that they had broken through. Groundhog pulled a she-vamp back into the building. She was trying to jump. May as well have let her. It was getting sunny outside.

The sight of a familiar face gave Brett pause. He stopped firing. And remembered.

Smiling. No, smirking. On his sister's arm. Brett hadn't liked him then. He was creepy. Too smooth. Too pale. Too…too…too…

Brett screamed. No. Roared. Like a monster himself. Corpsmen turned, as he charged after the vamp, who broke through the wall, leaving a hole that Brett vaulted through, dropping his shotgun.

He ran. Clawed himself over countertops, under tables, through a window into a next-door tenement close enough to jump to. He felt nothing else. He saw nothing else. Just the figure before him. Running. Panting even though he didn't need to pant. Brett didn't pant, even though he needed to. A reversal of roles. As the predator became the prey. And Brett thought of nothing else but blood. All the blood. Blood and fire.

Brett skidded to a halt as the vampire suddenly turned into a room. Dead-end. It turned. It was afraid. Like any cornered beast should be. It drew a knife.

Brett let out a primal roar and charged. The vampire hadn't fought fairly in his life before. And despite his dark curse, despite his mutations and un-life, Brett let the knife sink into the armour of his chest-plate. It stopped and the vampire let go, as Brett caught it by the throat. He didn't stop. He carried it, using the momentum of his rage to drive it into the wall. Again, and again. Plaster tore and bits of skin and hair stuck onto the wall. It wasn't enough.

Brett used his other hand to grab the vampire's hair and pulled it onto the ground. It still had some fight in it, but not enough. As it resisted, Brett rammed its head into the ground. It was dazed, but still wriggled.

Not enough.

Brett beat its head into the floor again. Again. Again. Again.

But it wasn't enough.

Its skull shattered. Blood and brain matter oozed from its eyes, nose and ears.

The force of Brett's grip on the creature's head crushed the now fragile skull even more. He kept driving its head. More and more. Never stopping. And it never stopped.

And it was never good enough.

Because they weren't coming back. They were never coming back. And Brett would never come back. Ever. Ever. Ever.

He only had hatred now.

Hatred because he loved them.

And monsters took them all away.

Tears fell in rivulets down his cheeks, mingling with the mulch that was left of the vampire. He barely heard the footsteps, cautious, behind him. His hands were sore. His arms were stiff. He kept pushing the flesh into the ground.

A hand touched his shoulder and he turned on the assailant, backing away and reaching for his knife with a bloody flesh covered hand.

His comrades looked…understanding. Sad. Angry. Despairing.

But they understood.

They knew.

Sirens in the distance.

Krieg, his faced covered in bloodstained bandages, stepped forward.

"Let's go, Corpsman."

Chapter 11. Clientele

I arrived back at Cindy's (or should I call it home?) at 3am. The lights were still on. I limped my way to the door and reached to put the keys in the lock. The door opened.

"Cindy," I said, smiling. And it was a genuine, if tired, smile.

"I see you are well," she commented, with a hint of accusation in her voice, but also of concern.

I must've looked a mess. Matted hair covered in necro-blood, dirt and ash covering my skin, and bruises everywhere. I felt great.

She made way to let me in.

"Take a seat so I can heal you, please," she said, as if from habit.

"No…" I blurted out. And then took a seat anyway. "I mean: no, thanks."

"You've been monster hunting." A statement, not a question.

"Zombie outbreak in the slums."

"And you're injured."

"Nothing severe. And I like it this way. I earned it. It reminds me of what I did. Of who I am."

She nodded. She seemed to understand.

She took a seat opposite me and tossed me a bottle of water. I caught it deftly, despite my injuries, and chugged. I deposited the empty bottle on the coffee table when I was done.

"I phoned Brett after I saw your note," she said, cupping her hands. She looked poised. She always looked poised. Even when she had vomit caked around her mouth after spell burn-out.

I winced. Brett. It seemed long ago, but it had only been hours. A lot of hours, but still.

"I thought you'd be with him. And your phone was off," she said.

"Brett…" I licked my dry lips and leaned forward, despite my tiredness. Cindy had reminded me of my concerns and even my accomplishment this night was overshadowed by my anxieties and uncertainties.

"Brett and I had a fight," I said.

She raised her eyebrow, looking quizzically at the blood on my shoes.

"No, no! Not that type of fight. An argument."

She sighed.

"What happened?"

"He wanted me to move in with him."

"And?"

"I refused?"

"And?" she pressed.

Remembering it made me angry. And frustrated. I clenched my fists.

"He mentioned Colin."

A silence fell. So silent that I could hear Duer snoring. Cindy must have set up his bird-house on the top shelf of the bookcase. His snoring sounded like a little drill.

Cindy nodded, slowly.

"I don't hate him," I said.

"I know you don't."

"But I'm angry with him."

"And you have every right to be."

I felt some anger rising at how nonchalant and calm Cindy seemed to be. But I couldn't be angry with her. She was letting me stay with her. I'd be on the streets if not for her. On the streets, or living with…

"I didn't want to move in with…it just didn't feel right."

Cindy smiled, slightly. "Two overgrown man-children living in an arsenal? I don't blame you. And you're welcome to stay here as long as you need."

"Thank you, Cindy. I really mean it. And I'll pay you what I owe as soon as I am able."

She waved away the comment.

"No. I'm serious. The second I can afford to do so, I'm paying rent. And if I find a new place, I'll pay you back-rent."

She sighed. "I'd argue, but it's pretty late. And I know you, Kat Drummond. And I know your honour is all."

I nodded, despite the hint of friendly mockery in her voice.

She stood and yawned.

"Sorry to keep you up."

Bags under her eyes, she smiled. "It's fine, Kat. I know this has been a hard day. For you. For him."

"Him?"

"Brett is an odd man, as you know. But he isn't a bad one."

"I know he isn't, but…"

"But he says stupid things and thinks stupid thoughts. But at the end of the day, he would fight the Titan for us. You know that?"

"I know." And I believed it.

"Be angry with him," she said. "It's healthy. But I ask you to forgive him. When you can. Because he deserves that much. And because you deserve it too."

Before I could question her cryptic words further, she waved me goodnight and disappeared into her room. I yawned myself and made my way into the bathroom. My shower was cold. On purpose. Then hot. I cleansed myself of dried blood and sweat, admired my new bruises and old scars, and made my way to the guest room. My room, now, I guess.

The light in my room had been left on. Boxes containing my meagre belongings were arrayed across the desk and floor. I would need to find space to store my books. In the morning. I stifled another yawn and noticed some blue clothes neatly laid out on the bed. My pyjamas. Tidily folded. I sniffed them. She had washed them as well.

I should have smiled. I normally had to handle my own laundry. Being here, with Cindy, life could become easier.

But I didn't smile. Tears welled up and streamed down my face. Treth didn't ask why. He felt it.

I loved Cindy for this. And I loved Charne for being the only mother I had left. But they were not and could never be my mom.

***

I dreamed of Colin. Of our happy times. Of our tender moments. I didn't dream of blood. I dreamed of joy. And that made my awakening the ever more painful.

***

I awoke to the sound of horse hooves on concrete. My window was closest to the street. Even so, I had slept through the cacophony of early morning traffic. Bleary-eyed, I checked my phone. 11am. I had slept long. Well, not too long considering when I fell asleep. I lifted myself out of bed, sluggish from my dreams. I heard typing in the other room. Cindy must still be home.

The clopping of hooves grew louder, and then stopped. The sound of the doorbell ringing was a surprising punctuation to the sound.

I heard Cindy open the door, and then muffled speaking. Curious, I opened my curtains just a fraction.

"Athena!" I gasped.

"No, that's a centaur," Treth said.

"Shush. I've never seen one in person before."

"Me neither. Get dressed so we can meet him."

"He's probably a client of Cindy's. May not be our place to talk to him."

"Never know that until we take the chance."

I considered Treth's words and felt his almost childlike excitement. He did a good job acting like an adult and dignified knight, but he was still a teenager from a backwater world.

I got dressed hastily and rushed to the bathroom to brush my teeth and hair (with different brushes).

"Hurry!" Treth begged, his knightly poise slipping.

At least partly presentable, I made my way towards the front door. Duer was watching from around the corner. I ignored him and approached Cindy, her back turned. I could only see the bottom half of the centaur's torso, and the lower horse-part of his body. He was wearing a shirt and brown jacket, but I could see the shape of his frame underneath. Sculpted abs and a demi-godly frame. Just like the myths.

Cindy turned at my approach.

"Good morning, Kat. You've got a guest."

I stopped, shocked. "Me?"

The centaur backed away and then leant down to look through the doorway. He was clean-shaven. If he was human, I'd put him at around his late twenties. He wore round glasses on a long nose and had a clean, long dark brown ponytail.

"Ms Drummond, I presume?"

"Yes." I said, dumbly.

He didn't seem to mind. He smiled warmly.

"I am Ipherios."

I exited the house and accepted his outstretched hand. It was subtle, but even his human-parts were slightly larger than a normal human. His hand almost engulfed mine, but his grip was gentle. He was a man who knew his own strength, so reined it in dramatically so as not to hurt anyone.

"Kat, Ipherios has a job for you," Cindy added.

"A job?" I didn't say this dumbly, but my scepticism was obvious. Why would a centaur want to hire me?

"I went to your old address, but the landlord chased me off with the threat of calling the police. As if asking after a tenant was a crime." His back leg stomped, subtly and irritably. "But one of the workers was polite enough to tell me that he heard your pixie talk about a Cindy. I guessed, rightly, that it must be the Cindy Giles."

"You flatter me," Cindy added, just short of a chuckle.

"Not at all," he said, serious. "Holy Light has done a lot for us. When not many would. My father came to this world as a foal and was chased as a beast. But Holy Light saw the value in his life, and gave him meaning."

"It was the right thing to do," Cindy said, flatly.

"But very few did it," Ipherios replied, and turned to me again. "Ms Drummond, we have needed you for days now, yet it seems you are no longer on the MonsterHunter App."

I frowned. "I am in the process of sorting that out."

"So, you are still a hunter?"

"If I can help it, yes."

He sighed with relief. "We were worried!"

"We?"

"Oh! Forgive me. I come representing the resident association of the New Altworld District in East Mannenberg. It's a predominantly non-human…um, you would say slum."

"Monster trouble? Undead?" I asked, immediately. Straight to business. Dealing with resident associations wasn't new. Even if the species of said resident association reps had been predominantly (read: 100%) human.

"Not undead, exactly," he said, averting his gaze and tapping his back hooves nervously.

"Kat is an undead specialist," Cindy added, placing her hands on her hips. I felt I didn't want to be stern with the centaur. His alien-ness not only intrigued me, but I found his face endearing. In a way, he reminded me of Colin.

"I know, I know. But…" I realised that the fidgeting of his back hooves was not just a sign of anxiety, but desperation. "Ms Drummond, you're our only hope."

"What is the monster, Ipherios? I'll do my best. I specialise in undead, but I've also killed vampires, drakes, demons, werewolves…"

"What about trolls?"

That stopped me.

"No," I almost whispered. "Not trolls."

He looked a little concerned.

"Trolls are high-level hunting material," Cindy said. "Agency stuff."

"None of the agencies will take it."

"That's to be expected," I answered Cindy's unspoken question. "Agencies seldom go into the slums. For the resources it'd take to kill a troll, it is seldom worth it for them. Which means…"

I looked at him accusingly, but also somewhat pityingly. "You can't afford to hire troll hunters."

"Ah…"

"Which means," Cindy butted in. "She isn't doing the job."

"Cindy!"

"No, Kat. If they can't afford your services, then they can't hire you."

"Cindy, I need the money."

"Ms Drummond!" Ipherios said loudly, and then straightened his glasses nervously. "We…we can afford it."

"Why not hire an agency, then?" I asked.

"The agencies are refusing to help. No matter the pay."

"How much did you offer them."

"$1000. And help to transport and sell the body."

"$1000?" I asked, while doing a quick calculation. From what I knew, the money in troll hunting was in the body. Could fetch anything between $20k to $30k from it. The difficult part was securing the kill. Trolls didn't only hit hard, their hides were rock-solid. Old trolls could resist shots from a tank. And if you managed to break the skin, the flesh tended to just knit itself back together. And it wasn't like fighting vampires or werewolves. Silver and fire didn't stop the body from growing back. Only thing that could stop a troll was complete dismemberment, and then being encased in concrete so it couldn't grow its limbs back. Or, letting it out in the sun so its flesh would turn to stone.

That was the simpler option.

"Where is this troll?"

"Kat! You can't be seriously considering this. $1000 is a tenth of the agency rate for a troll."

"I am, Cindy. For the body. If I sell it, I'll be able to pay you years' worth of rent. Or get my own place."

"You're not a troll hunter!"

"And I wasn't a vampire hunter, or a demon hunter, or an undead hunter."

I turned to face her.

"I'll find a way to do this. And I'll make sure I come back alive. I owe you for taking me in. And I'll repay my debts."

"You've stayed for one night!"

"With the promise of many nights to come! And that's worth something." I smiled, to try reassure her. "I'll be okay."

"The troll is located in a tunnel system near the neighbourhood. It's the best way to get in and out of the district, and its raised travel times by two hours or more."

"You want to risk Kat's life over the daily commute?!"

"No, Ms Giles," he said, seriously. "I want to hire her so the troll will stop coming into our neighbourhood at night and eating our foals and young."

That silenced her. He looked at me, earnestly and with the desperation of not only a neighbourhood rep, but as a brother, son and father.

"I know this isn't an easy task, Ms Drummond. And please do not think that we are like many, who blindly throw the lives of heroes at the monsters of the world. I ask you to do this with the solemn realisation that I may be sending you to die. But I also send you because I know I must. For my foals' sake. For my neighbour's' sake. If not you, we are not sure if anyone else can save us."

Cindy was about to say something, but it seemed his words had moved her. She crossed her arms and turned away, but I did see the hint of moisture in her eyes.

"I'll do it," I said, clenching my fists. "Give me time to prepare, and transport."

"Thank you, Ms Drummond!" There were tears in his eyes.

"Thank me after that troll's dead. And call me Kat."

***

"If you insist on running this foolish mission, then you need help," Cindy said, after Ipherios had left, arranging to pick me up the day after tomorrow. I didn't see how he had

121

arrived here himself. I guessed some sort of trailer or truck. Unless he had spent the entire day galloping from the slums. Well, I've done similar trips and I don't have half a horse for a body.

"Help from whom?" I asked, my stomach grumbling. "Duer! Stop annoying Alex."

Duer, who was suspiciously hovering near my cat, crossed his arms behind his back and whistled while floating away. Alex flicked his tail irritably and renewed his nap.

Cindy made her way to the kitchen and I followed. Cindy's laptop was on the counter. She was typing out an email and before I could recall that reading someone's work was rude, I noticed that it was an email to an orphanage. I knew Cindy worked with orphanages a lot, but not exactly the extent. There was a lot about Cindy that I didn't know.

Cindy passed me the cereal box (corn flakes) and I prepared a bowl for myself. She typed away while half-sipping a coffee. When I was done, we renewed the conversation.

"Help from whom?" I repeated. "I think I've overused my credits after what we did at the Garce Manor."

"You have endless credits with one man," she said, clicking a button on screen and then closing the laptop.

I shifted on my seat, uncomfortable.

"Perhaps we should get his help," Treth offered.

"I…I don't think I'm ready. Just yet."

"Brett would help you. Angry or not," Cindy replied.

"But do I have a right to ask him? I haven't forgiven him yet. Also…I feel a bit uncomfortable asking for favours from those two. I got them fired, after all."

"It's much more complicated than that, but you know that Brett would still help?"

And that's what made it worse. I knew he would help, but I also knew I was still angry with him. Perhaps, because I suspected he did like me. And that I didn't know if I liked him that way back.

"I don't want to give him false hope," I said, aloud.

"False hope?"

"I…I think he likes me."

"Well, duh. But that's his business. You can still be friends with him. Or more?"

"That's the thing. I don't know if there could be more. Not now. Not with Colin so recent in my memory."

I looked down at my empty cereal bowl. Treth felt my sadness and echoed it.

"I still love him, Cindy. And I don't know if I'll love anyone else. And I like Brett, I really do, but I'm not sure if I can ever grow the same feelings for him that I had for Colin."

There was a long silence as Cindy absorbed my words.

Finally, she sighed. "I'd like to tell you that you'll eventually forget Colin. And that you will find love again, but I can't be a hypocrite."

I looked up, questioningly. She sighed again, but much more forlornly.

"Nothing is certain in this chaotic game of relationships. We fall in and out of love, or we meet someone and never get over them. Even when we really should. Even when you know they aren't coming back. And it isn't something we can rationalise. There's no handbook for it. Everyone's experience is different. But what I can do is give you advise based on what I've seen in my ancient few decades on this Earth.

"Don't feel you need to forget about Colin. And don't tell yourself you aren't allowed to love another. There will never be another Colin, but there doesn't need to be. And as long as there is a Kat, that Kat can try to find love again. If that's what she wants."

"But that's the thing, Cindy. I don't know if that's what I want."

She smiled, sadly.

"And you won't for a while. But if you do or don't, it shouldn't stop you from being friends with Brett. Or at least colleagues. He's a good friend and a good hunter."

"I know…but…"

"You need space."

I nodded.

She sighed.

"Well, I've done stupider things when I was your age. Like befriending a sleazy angel. And you probably can handle this troll."

"It can't be worse than the Necrolord's abhorrent."

She nodded in agreement. "You have a knack for hitting far above your weight category."

"Thanks. And this won't be any different."

She creased her forehead and reached to grab my hand.

"Just…Kat…promise me you'll be careful."

I nodded. "I will."

Chapter 12. A Bridge Too Far

I was in a district of the slums, during the middle of the day, yet the eerie quiet made it seem more like a ghost town. The troll had already depopulated much of the area. Deaths led to evacuations. Those who could not leave, acted only a little better than dead – becoming prisoners in their own homes. There was an oppressive quality to the dirty air of New Altworld District (or NAD, but don't tell the residents that). One that I knew too well from slums overrun by the undead. Fear choked the air, adding to the already toxic hue of physical smog and weyline decay. Yet, in undead slums, I was usually welcomed by the comforting sounds of gurgling, growling, chomping and the usual sound effects of peckish corpses. Here, I was greeted by…nothing.

"Who still lives here?" I asked Ipherios. He was dismounting a trailer, driven by an elf. While I had met elves before, I found myself somewhat cold towards this elf. Not this elf in particular. She was inoffensive. A bit quiet. But with what was happening in New Zealand, and with what had happened to my aunt…

Rational me knows I shouldn't blame elves in Hope City for the actions of New Sintar, but humans can often be irrational. When I saw this elf at the wheel, I couldn't help but think about other elves. Much less peaceful elves. I chose to stay quiet, checking over my equipment in the back of the car.

Among my usual gear, using Brett's swords, I had managed to procure a magically-hardened vial. Troll-hide was strong. Too strong often even for bullets, sometimes. But it wasn't invulnerable. In researching trolls, I read about their role in the ecosystem. In particular: their natural predator. They had only one. Drakes. And of drakes, a specific breed of acid spewing drakes that saliva softened, and melted troll hide like butter, letting claws and teeth, or in my case, bullets and blade pass through and pierce the juicy bits within. With a loan (I insisted) from Cindy, I purchased a vial of drake acid from an alchemist and secured it in the inner pocket of my salamander coat. Even if I could pierce the hide, however, trolls were notorious for their regeneration. If you somehow managed to lop the arm off a troll, expect it to grow right back. Silver wouldn't do you any good, like it did with vampires. Try to sprinkle silver dust on a troll's stump and all you'd get is a sparkly troll arm. This made my job awfully difficult. But I knew that trolls had been killed in the past. Quite often. And by humans.

Which meant they had a weakness. There was a well-known weakness. When in the purifying rays of sunlight, trolls turned to stone. Something Tolkien got right in his very much pre-Cataclysm masterpiece. But I couldn't turn this troll to stone. First, it was deep within the dark confines of this tunnel. Second, if the body was turned to stone, I couldn't sell it. Troll statues didn't fetch much on the market. But there was another weakness, and as is the cliché, that weakness was the brain.

"Just like killing undead," Treth commented. I had to agree. Destroy the brain. Destroy its ability to think and regenerate. Easy-peasy. Sprinkle some acid on its head, skewer it. Back home in time for coffee. And I could even pay Cindy for it. Or even buy the coffee myself! The thought of going grocery shopping had never been so exciting.

"Not many," Ipherios answered me, bringing me back to the present. "We've got a neighbourhood militia that watches this entrance, but there's not much we can do when it attacks. We often evacuate. Those who lived next to the tunnel either left the district or…"

He didn't finish. Didn't need to.

"Any details on the layout of the tunnel, Ipherios?"

The elf handed me a small folded piece of paper. I opened it. It was a map of the area, with a detailed sketch of the tunnel. And it was just that. A tunnel. Nothing too impressive. It was built through a jagged hill, topped by ruins that nobody had had a mind to clear. The tunnel itself was just a long winding stretch, no detours, until it connected with the highway on the other side.

"Easy enough," I said. "It won't be able to hide."

"Same goes for us," Treth added.

"I suspect that map may be outdated," Ipherios said. "But it's the best we have."

"Outdated? It's dated this year."

"Before the troll arrived. And I doubt that he would have just left it as is."

Ipherios pointed to a building behind me. I noticed now that the wall had been torn open.

"Trolls like to recraft the world to their whims. They aren't content to just be a part of something. Everything must change."

"You know a lot about trolls, Ipherios?"

He seemed to blush. His tail swished. "A bit. But not enough. Not enough to change anything."

He frowned near the end of his statement. His mind seemed to wander.

"I'll do what I can," I said, breaking him out of his reverie.

He nodded and stomped his front hoof. "We will wait for your return."

I did a final check of my equipment, ensured my sword-belt was on tight (but not too tight), did some stretches, and made my way to the tunnel entrance.

"You ready for this?" Treth asked.

"As ready as I can ever be," I whispered. And I had to be ready. This was my chance to get back in the fight. To reclaim my dignity. To kill monsters again. And, more important than all that, it was time to save some people.

"And Treth," I added, entering the darkness of the tunnel. "Not to seem arrogant but recall who has beaten not only a Vampire God, but an Archdemon."

"We didn't beat the Archdemon."

"Sure, we did. He stopped trying to kill us, didn't he?"

"I'm not sure that counts as a victory."

I grinned. "Let's just agree to disagree."

The light of the outside was still on my back, but the darkness ahead was unabating. A veritable black hole, absorbing all the light ahead of it. I would have feared it. But I've faced worse darkness before. I had plunged into it. And in some cases, befriended it.

The darkness of this tunnel would not deter me. What it contained, on the other hand…

No! I stopped.

"Kat?"

The light of the entrance was far enough back that I doubted Ipherios or the elf could see me pause.

"You can go back, Kat. I won't think any less of you. And you shouldn't think any less of yourself if you do."

I clenched my fists and peered through the darkness. My coat glowed a warm sombre orange. It pulsed. Breathed. As if alive. Well, it was alive. In its own way.

"No. We're doing this. We have a plan. A good plan."

Treth nodded.

"And even if I didn't beat that damn demon, I did beat that damn Ancient!"

Treth glowed with a hint of pride.

I renewed my march. Through the darkness, until the heat of the outside dissipated and was replaced by the cold confines of concrete and almost subterranean moisture. My body was kept warm by my coat, but my face felt the icy chill of a place that the sun never touched.

"Trolls can see in the dark, Kat. May as well use your headtorch."

I activated a torch attached to my helmet. My old face-plate made by Pranish, combined with a construction hard-hat. The white light pooled in a beam, stopping short of the distant dark, but illuminating the torn-up road, broken lights, ripped up piping, and bones. A lot of bones. I kneeled down to examine a pile. Not a single human. But I couldn't be sure it was human. The bones were in disparate piles, strewn across the tunnel. I lifted what could have been a femur, but half of it had been chewed into mulch.

"Better keep your sword and vial ready," Treth said, his voice shaky.

"Scared, Sir-Knight?" I tried to be cocky, but my voice also shook.

"Me? I'm dead. What do I have to be scared of."

I snorted, amused, and stood up.

Further into the tunnel, I saw evidence of shredded clothes. Some were recognisable. Jeans, t-shirts, jackets. Others were just torn up fabric, caught on jagged pieces of concrete and metal. There were dark patches on the clothing. I didn't look close enough to confirm which bodily excretion was the culprit.

I had not made it far, but the light from the entrance was already out of view. I must have passed the first bend. And still no sign of the troll. I hated this. The worst part of any mission was that anticipation. That waiting to kill or die. Fights weren't a big deal. You were too busy fighting to dread. But when you were walking towards a fight, you had an awfully long time to ponder.

My dangerous thoughts were stopped by a thud. In the distance.

"You hear that?"

I raised my finger to my lips to quieten my companion.

Silence.

And then…another thud. And another. Rhythmic. Footsteps. Heavy footsteps. And because I doubted an ogre or giant was in this tunnel, it could only be the troll. I drew my sword in my right-hand and the acid vial in my left. I walked softly, but every scrape and scratch on the surface made me wince. But the sound of heavy footfalls didn't stop and sent minor vibrations throughout the tunnel.

And as I drew closer, I encountered the worst thing of all. The smell. Oh, gods, Athena, Rifts and Vortex! The smell. It was worse than any zombie horde I'd encountered. Worse than the dirtiest of gym lockers. It was as if the pungency of death had decided to ferment in manure, to make itself presentable to the grandfather of neglected public bathrooms.

Succinctly, it smelled like troll.

I had to stop for breath but breathing now meant breathing in the stench. I covered my mouth and nose with my coat sleeve. It heated up, dissipating the odour as the flames absorbed the gases. This coat had endless uses! I felt bad for killing it.

I caught my breath and continued.

Thump…

Thump….

It stopped.

And just as it had become its loudest.

I peered into the darkness where my light couldn't reach, walking with even steps and my sword ready. The edge of my light caught something. My heart stopped. I paused and drifted my light over it again.

An indentation in the wall.

No, a cave entrance. I sniffed and regretted it.

The smell was coming from inside.

I snuck to the wall and sidled to the edge to peer inside.

The cave looked old. But the hole was new. Perhaps, the troll had re-opened the cave? As a sort of lair.

I took a deep breath of at least semi-clean air and entered the cave. It wound and twisted, not allowing me to see clearly what was ahead or what I was leaving behind. The stench only grew greater and ranker. Until…

"Nothing!"

The room was a dome, sprinkled with bones, like everywhere else, but also what seemed to be piles of sludge. I suspected I knew what they were, and it is not in polite company that I shall explain further.

Besides that small evidence of troll, I found none, and turned back.

"Must be further up. Perhaps there are more caves like this? The centaur said that trolls like to re-shape their surroundings. Not sure why that's so odd, actually. Humans of Earth and Avathor both do the same," Treth said, seeming talkative from nerves. I didn't respond. Stealth-mode, and all that.

I exited the cave and was thankful to be in the more open air of the tunnel, where at least a slight breeze would push away some of the stench. But the breeze that had been coming from the entrance to my left had stopped.

"Kat…"

I turned my head slowly. As I felt a warm gust of air on my flesh. No. Breath.

The troll bent down so its head, the size of a beer keg, was level with mine. It…he…had a massive grin on his face, revealing a row of crooked, sharp teeth, mottled with blood, bone and bits of clothing. His eyes were a sickly yellow and, contrasting with his dark grey skin and patches of stone-like dark growths, was a head of stringy, greasy black hair.

I froze. He was a metre away yet felt only a handspan. He breathed again, creating a competitor for the stench of his bathroom.

"You…" he bellowed, drawing out the word long as he struggled to enunciate it. I heard a crunch as he lifted a massive three-fingered fist and pointed a single finger at me.

"Pay toll," he boomed.

Stunned, I faced the beast, putting one foot back.

"Toll?" I asked, simply.

He nodded, eagerly, and revealed his other hand. He pointed at his palm.

"Toll!"

"What gives you the authority to toll this road?" I asked, accusation in my voice. I sounded like a schoolteacher, or someone asking to speak to the manager at a restaurant.

He squinted at my question.

"Big word. No. Toll?"

I sighed, taking another step back, subtly.

"Do you own this road?"

He considered the question, and then nodded. Like an ape in a cartoon.

"Do you have the paperwork to prove this claim?"

He considered me, closing his mouth and seeming to frown. I jumped out of the way, just in time, as he smashed his fist into the ground.

"Big word no like!"

"Fine! Fine!"

He seemed to calm.

"I hope you know what you're doing, Kat."

Did I? I took a quick examination of the troll. It was around 3 to 4 metres tall. Perhaps more. It was hunched over, so it was hard to tell.

"You pay toll?"

"Yes. I pay toll."

It grinned again, its grotesque maw splitting its large head in two.

"What's the toll?" I asked.

It whispered, its voice still booming throughout the tunnel.

"Flesh."

I dove backwards, tripping over some bones and my back colliding into the wall. The troll's fist landed with a crunch and boom where I had just been standing.

"To your feet, Kat!"

"Like I don't know that!"

I pulled myself to my feet, just as the troll swung in again. My knees already bent, I jumped, narrowly missing the rocky flesh of the monster by a hairsbreadth. I even felt the air move below me.

"Kat…"

"I know!"

"The vial!"

Oh…

I didn't know.

My left hand was empty. Only the hand-strap and hand-guard kept my grip on the sword.

"Toll!" the troll yelled with glee. I heard the crack of stony flesh and bone and felt the whoosh, before ducking under his blow and feeling the crunch of his hand into the solid wall, leaving a giant fist sized dent.

"By his feet!" Treth yelled.

From my vantage point crawling along the ground, I saw something glassy and filled with green liquid reflect the light of my flashlight.

I pulled myself forwards, as the troll shifted his footing, kicking it further away.

"Play nice, flesh!"

I gritted my teeth.

"I'll play nice, alright!"

I rolled onto my feet and slid past the troll's ankles, slicing at it. My blade slid off like I was trying to cut a boulder.

"Ah, not like hunting undead, then," Treth said.

"More like hunting mimics," I panted.

The troll brought its foot down hard, picking up dust and debris and sending a shockwave that knocked me back.

"How'd we kill that?"

"I let it eat me."

"Oh…"

"Flesh! EAT!"

"Shut up, shit-face."

"Flesh rude!"

He had that right. I didn't try deflecting its three-finger grab, rather spinning like a coy dancer to avoid its touch.

"See it, Treth?"

"I not Treth. I troll."

"Shut up."

He roared, sounding more beast than simpleton now. Seemed I'd pissed it off.

"I can't, Kat!" Treth said. "I think the beast smashed it."

"That's enchanted glass, Treth. It'd take magic to break it."

"Then he's buried it."

"Fuck," I swore. That was my only plan. Without the acid, I couldn't kill it. Or could I?

I looked the troll up and down, as he smashed both his fists into the ground like an enraged gorilla and peered at me. Whenever his gaze settled, I spun, crouched and dove in another direction, circling him. His growl sent shimmers through the floor. He wasn't so talkative anymore.

I wanted to preserve his body but killing him was more important. For everyone. And most particularly – me. And that left me with one final choice.

"Oi, shit-face!"

The troll stopped and stared at me, its at least vaguely intelligent features looking completely animalistic now as it listened to me.

"You want your toll?"

"Toll?!!?" it growled, roared and coughed all at the same time.

"Then come and take it!"

I sprinted as fast as I could the way I had come, hoping my memory and body-compass was correct. As I had hoped, the troll came roaring after me, beating on the asphalt and turning the remains of its previous *tolls* into dust and mulch.

"Direct sunlight," Treth reminded me. "That means all the way out."

Like he needed to remind me!

I didn't turn around to see if the monster was still following me. I didn't need to. I could hear his grunting, smell his sweat and hear the booming of his hastened steps.

Just a little bit farther!

My legs started to ache. Not from the exertion. I'd done this plenty of times before. I must have twisted or injured them during the tussle. I kept swinging my arms, furiously pumping. The huffs and puffs of the troll came closer and closer.

And light.

In the distance. Oh, sweet Athena! And the troll was still on my tail. Just a little stretch. Closer. Closer.

I kept the sprint, renewed by the light from the outside. The sight of a centaur and parked car, shanties and torn up road. I was going to make it. I was going to make it!

"Kat!" Treth yelled. I felt his intent and turned back.

The troll was gone.

Stunned, I searched through the darkness for the hulking beast. When had his grunts stopped? When had the bones stopped crunching?

The clanking of metal stopped me from my search.

"Kat! The entrance!"

I turned back towards the light, just as darkness enveloped it and a loud cacophony of metal fell upon the ground. My flashlight bounced off a thick layer of corrugated iron. A solid metal gate.

I realised that I wasn't the only hunter here. I was the prey. And I'd fallen into the monster's trap.

I realised that I was breathing. Fast. Hard. On the verge of panic. I kept my back to the gate, knowing the troll couldn't come from that direction, and faced my head-flashlight in every direction, scanning hastily for my hunter. I saw outlines. It moved! No. Shadows. Bones. Someone banged their fist on the gate. I wish they wouldn't. I needed to hear. But hear…

Thuds! No. Imagined it.

I backed slowly and slowly towards the gate, drawing both my swords. I startled myself with the ring of metal and felt Treth's distress merge with my own.

Where was he? Where was the troll?

I stepped back another step and stopped. As I collided with the hard surface, my coat exploded into a pillar of flames, sending forth a pyre that lit up the area, and temporarily blinded the troll looming over me.

I instinctively slashed a wide arc towards the troll while diving away from its blind grasping. The impact of my steel on the rock-flesh sent ringing through my bones and my teeth chattering.

"Run!"

I did so, turning on my heels and sprinting the other way. The other entrance. It had to be open. I had to get through. Even if it meant dodging highway traffic.

I felt a whoosh of air as a swipe almost took me out. The second grasp did. I felt the tip of its fingers brush against my leg, sending me spiralling down the tunnel, smashing into bones and debris. I tried to stand, but my leg hurt fiercely. I craned my neck up towards the troll, easily standing at its full height at about 5 or 6 metres tall, the flames from my coat creating an orange glow that made the monster look demonic. He rammed his fist into the wall and pulled out a twisted iron pipe. He swung down on me and I managed to roll out of the way, a small dent left in the concrete where I was a second ago. He pulled back for another blow.

I'm an idiot. An arrogant fool. And now I was going to die for it.

Something hit the troll in the face and stuck there. It looked like a javelin. He dropped his arm, pipe in hand. His rage seemed to have abated. With his free hand, he pulled out the javelin and stared at the tip. It exploded.

The troll cried out in pain, covering his face and dropping the pipe with a loud bang.

"Get it back to the gate!" Brett shouted, from the darkness.

I didn't delay, despite my surprise, and managed to force myself through the pain in my leg. The troll was still reeling from the shock, but he'd recover. If I let him.

I took a deep breath, apologised to future me that would have to deal with my exacerbated injuries, and took a running jump. For a second, I soared, and then grabbed hold of the troll's stringy hair. He tried to swat me, but I managed to swing around, using my momentum to land on the back of his neck and straddle him like a horse.

He pulled both his hands away from his eyes to get me off. I grinned, just a little bit sadistically, and used the opening to drive both my swords into the creature's eyes. He screamed just as deeply as he roared and was stuck between trying to claw my swords out of his eyes while shaking me off. I twisted the hilts, using them as guiding rods, and turned the troll back towards the gate.

I heard boots running, just ahead.

"Jump on one!" Brett yelled, exertion in his voice as he sprinted away from the blind, raging troll that I was leading.

The troll, hearing the voice, didn't need my coaxing so much to charge head first towards the gate.

"Three!" Brett yelled.

My coat ignited in force, singing the troll's hand as he tried to swat at me. I stabbed further into its eye as punishment.

"Two!"

I eased my skewering of its eye. The gate was just ahead. The troll was charging at full speed.

"One!"

I pulled out the swords and kick-jumped off the troll's back. Brett caught me in his arms, and I saw him click a button on a remote just as he did.

The gate exploded, allowing the troll to pass through it. Ipherios sprinted out of the way of the flailing troll, just as his eyes grew back, and he peered into the sun.

He looked back at us, desperately, and tried to run towards us, as his foot turned to stone, and then his leg. His torso collapsed to the ground, as he clawed his way towards the darkness. He had no grin now. His monstrous mouth was stuck in a look of extreme horror and desperation. His hand turned to stone, before his very eyes. To the last moment, his expression was one of desperation. I don't think he had an ounce of recognition of his own evil. That this was justice. He was a monster. And monsters only think about themselves.

Silence fell as the troll could no longer scream. I felt Brett's rapid heartbeat and my own in response. I looked up at him, and him down at me.

His gaze was one of extreme relief, but also something else. A tenderness I had seen before. I don't know what he saw, even when I took my face-plate off for air. For I did not know what was going through my own head.

He opened his mouth to speak, and my breath caught in my throat at the anticipation.

"You smell like troll shit." He grinned.

I shoved him onto the ground, while laughing and wincing at the pain in my leg. And then I hugged him tightly, as we lay on the ground, surrounded by bones.

Chapter 13. Agency

"So, we're down two sticks of explosives, a vial of drake acid, and you needed bone regeneration?" Guy asked, rhetorically and just a bit accusingly.

"Cindy did the last for free," I added.

"And you two still couldn't preserve the body for the real pay-out."

"The centaur managed to get us an extra $500," Brett replied.

"We blow $500 on toying with ghouls, Brett."

Guy sighed, weighed down with resignation. I saw the fires of another rant in the usually calm hunter, but this entire ordeal, and the fact that he hadn't gone hunting for weeks, had damaged him. Made him angry. As Brett had said before, Guy needed the hunt, just as much as we did. In a way, I think he envied Brett and me for going without him.

"We technically profited," I said. "Sure, we lost out on the body-fee, but our biggest costs were some explosives that you needed to dump anyway before Drakenbane remembered you had them."

"Supplies aren't the only cost in this game, Kat," Cindy added, sitting with her arms and legs crossed on her armchair. We were using her home as a base of operations for the troll hunt debriefing. Even if only Brett and I had been involved. Well, Cindy and Guy were technically investors, as they provided some materials. Even if Guy hadn't known until he phoned Cindy and found Brett by my side as Cindy regrew my muscle tissue and damaged bones.

"I know," I replied. "Labour, as well. But this has never been an industry that pays well per hour."

"It's more than that. When you go out on a hunt, you aren't only putting a price on your time and your equipment. You're putting a price on your life. When you and Brett are pleased with a measly $1500, you are saying that your lives, collectively, are only worth that much."

I shrugged. "If that's what the market decides."

Cindy let out a sigh of resignation that put Guy's to shame. Now Guy's turn again, he turned to his friend.

"And you! You've been grinning like an idiot this entire time."

"Really?" Brett asked, still grinning. "It's just that…it felt good."

"Kat almost getting killed, and then you almost getting killed?"

"Well, partly. The hunt. Doing it again. And, saving Kat was also a bonus. Got to feel like a knight in shining armour."

He winked at me.

"I was handling it!" I exclaimed.

He rolled his eyes, amused. "Right!"

"Handling it or not," Guy butted in. "Don't get a taste for it. We're blacklisted. This was a fluke. A fluke that we can't rely on."

He slumped down into the couch.

"Face it. We need to move on. I'm glad you two had a fun, but it's time we grow up and find something else to do."

A sombre silence fell over us. Nobody argued with Guy. Could we argue with him? He was right. This troll hunt was a fluke. And a semi-illegal one at that. Monster hunting required a license, or at least working for someone or something with a license. Brett and I were technically criminals for being paid to kill that troll. Well, it wouldn't be our first offence. Far from it.

"Is there any more coffee?" Brett asked, his grin gone, and his tone subdued.

Cindy shook her head.

"I'll go get some." I needed to get out of the house. Away from the reminder that my way of life may very well be coming to an end.

Cindy stood to retrieve her wallet. I raised my hand to stop her.

"I'll use some of our reward. May as well use it for something."

She nodded and I left the house. The sounds of birds and traffic greeted me upon my exit, and I released a heavy sigh.

"There has to be something we can do," Treth said. "We can't just stop killing monsters."

"I don't know, Treth," I whispered, and began the walk to the shop. I was wearing my salamander coat and its flaming aura pulled a few glances from passers-by. I didn't mind the looks. They looked at me because I was odd. Because I wasn't like them. Because I could never be like them.

And I didn't want to be like them.

I was me.

And I was a monster hunter.

I clenched my fist and gritted my teeth, watching my boots, dark with dried necro-blood, stomping on cracks in the sidewalk. How many hunts had they faced? How many times had I almost died?

And what would I do without all this?

"You're not alone, you know." Treth said. "The others, they're the same. I can see it. They're like us. Brett, Guy, Cindy…they're hunters too. And they must be thinking the same things as us."

"That there is no life without the hunt?"

"That this is our life. And that we're in this together."

I stopped. A car slowed down, its driver seeing if I was okay, before speeding up again. I looked up at the sky. It was a clear, summer day. Some drakes were flying high above, where they wouldn't disturb anyone. There was a pack of them. Working together to ward off larger predators and bring down difficult prey. It would take a full squad from Drakenbane to take them down when they decided to land and nest.

It suddenly hit me, and I turned around and sprinted back to Cindy's. It was so simple! I was embarrassed that none of us had thought about it before.

I burst back into the house, panting and dripping with sweat.

"Kat? That was quick." Cindy raised her eyebrow, quizzically. She examined my arms. "Where's the coffee?"

"It's simple!" I announced, loudly. Stunning them.

"What is?" Brett asked, visibly concerned.

"Cindy, have you been blacklisted like the rest of us?"

She raised her eyebrow, thought about it for a second, and opened her mouth in an *oh*. I saw the twinkle in her eye. She had figured it out.

"I'm not listed."

"Really?" Guy asked. "How did you freelance with us?"

"I'm not listed, but I am licensed. Through Heiliges Licht."

"Wait…that means you've got an agency license. Like we used to have."

She slowly smiled. "Better. I'm not just an associate of Heiligeslicht, remember? I'm a Paladin. In essence, I am a special operations member for the Association."

"Which means…?"

"I can use my license at my discretion. And I answer to no one but the Order-Meister."

"So, you can still hunt monsters. Mind subsidising us?" Brett commented, wryly.

"She won't need to," I replied. "Because if she has a license, she can extend the rights of the license to the rest of us, as her subordinates."

"Just like an agency," Guy said, holding his chin, thoughtfully. I saw his mental gears turning. I couldn't help but smile.

"Exactly like an agency! And more than that, she can get us listed not as freelancers, but as an agency."

"Which means big bucks." Brett was already grinning ear to ear, gazing at me admiringly. Not my looks, but at what I'd figured out. I had found a way to get us out of this hole.

"Would we be able to handle agency-level jobs?" Guy asked.

"We destroyed a vampire syndicate. And Kat killed their god," Brett said. "We can more than handle it."

"Wait, what is this about a god?" Cindy asked. She didn't know the story.

"Cindy, what do you think?" I asked, turning to her. "It's your license. You who will be running the agency. It's up to you if you're okay with this. I know you aren't a monster hunter anymore. But…"

She raised her hand to shush me. "Enough, Kat. You should know me by now. And you should know what it means to be a purifier – for me, at least. We're not so different from monster hunters and, I understand what you guys must be going through. So, to cut a long explanation short, I'm in."

I considered hugging Cindy suddenly and tightly, but was beaten by Guy, who embraced her in the most open display of emotion I've ever seen from the hunter.

"Thank you! Thank you!" he repeated, holding Cindy tightly. She was blushing, while quietly replying. "It's nothing. It's nothing."

Finally, Guy released her, and I could guess that he was blushing himself, but his skin tone made it hard to tell.

"Well, there's one very important thing to do before we proceed," Brett said, brushing off the possible awkwardness and warmth of Guy's display. He grinned. "If we're starting an agency, we need a name."

"The Crusaders," Treth suggested. I repeated it to the group.

Brett's grin became mischievous. "Kat's Crusaders. I like it."

It was my turn to blush. "It's Cindy's outfit!"

"No, no, no!" she said, rapidly. Her poise had been stripped away slightly by Guy's actions. "I'll help you guys set it up and I'll help in some hunts, but I can't lead this. I'm not a leader."

"You led that old squad of Conrad's well enough," Guy replied.

She snorted. "Far from it! That group never had a leader. Well, except for Tom…but…"

She trailed off and began to look sombre.

"We don't need a leader," I said, distracting her from reverie. "We've got our skills, our specialties, and we trust each other. Cindy, if you don't want to lead us, I think that's fine. We don't need a leader. We post up the listing on MonsterSlayer App, we pick the hunts we each want to do and we collaborate when necessary. At the end of the day, this is just a way for us to get back in the hunt."

Brett stood, his expression suddenly earnest. "It's more than that, Kat. The other agencies…they don't know what really matters. You said it yourself. Yeah, profits matter. The bottom line keeps us hunting. But at the end of the day, we're here for one reason - to slay monsters. No matter how low the bids. No matter the client. If it deserves to die, we need to kill it."

"If I may add to that," Cindy said. "And to add a core principle to the newly formed Kat's Crusaders..."

"I didn't..." I began before I was cut off.

"We don't just exist to kill things, Brett. And I want to make that clear. We hunt because, at the end of the day, it saves someone. And that is why I'm a purifier and not just a healer. Because sometimes you have to slay something to save someone."

I nodded. I had realised this recently. And I knew how important it was. I hoped Guy and Brett realised the same.

"We're in this for three things, lady and gentlemen," I said, raising a finger and counting up. "For profit, for the hunt, and to save those who need to be saved."

"Sounds like decent reasons to crusade," Guy commented, grinning now. I think I'd gotten him out of his slump.

"We're gonna need to finalise another name, sometime."

"Nah, I like it the way it is," Brett said.

"Me too," Treth added.

I sighed, and my three friends, now colleagues, laughed. I finally smiled and joined them.

The crusade had begun again.

Chapter 14. Friend Far Away

"Kat..." the wind whispered into my ear. I stood in an empty field, surrounded by dark green grass as far as the eye could see. The sky was grey and held hints of rain, yet the air was dry, and the temperature muted between hot and cold. I smelled death.

"Kat..." the wind bellowed again.

"Treth, do you hear that?" I whispered.

No reply. I sent out my senses, seeing if I could detect him in his chamber. He wasn't there. Suddenly, I felt a gaping hole in myself, as if I had lost a part of my own soul. Where was Treth? Where was my knight?

"Kat!" the wind yelled, but it wasn't the wind. It was Candace.

"Candace? What is going on?"

"The Mentor, Kat," she half-screamed, half-whispered. "He is back. The man who killed your family."

"Where are you? What is this?"

"I need to hide, Kat. I can't let him have me again. He can't have me or your eye."

"What do you mean?"

"The eye connects us. He won't want that. He doesn't want anything he can't control."

"Candace! Come back. We can help."

"He will know! I can't. I need to run. Far, far, far…"

Lightning struck the field, and torrents of rain hit the Earth. I heard hissing as the rain pelted onto my salamander coat. I had barely noticed it before. It felt like a second-skin here.

"Candace! Calm down. I'm here."

"No, no…don't be here. He's coming for me. And then he'll be coming for you!"

"Who is he? What are you talking about?"

"The man who will remake the world, Kat. My mentor. The man who ordered the death of my father. The man who killed your parents. The Mentor! Who struck your soul asunder."

She screamed.

"Candace! Candace! Speak to me. Don't let the madness take over again. We went through too much together. We're sisters, Candace! And I'll protect you no matter what."

As abruptly as it had started, the storm abated. Candace didn't reply, but I felt her presence.

"Kat," she whispered. "I can't come back. Just yet. But I will. Nearer the end. When we can both take our revenge…"

***

Revenge.

I had tasted it already. The blood of a hated werewolf. It had felt good to strike him down. Good to see him suffer. But that was while I had been angry. While the rage and hate fuelled me.

I don't think I hated Andy anymore. I didn't regret killing him. But it was hard to hate a corpse. Well, hard to hate corpses that weren't walking around.

But that's just it. He wasn't walking around. He was dead. By my hand. I had taken my revenge. And it was sweet, for a time, but it didn't bring Colin back. And it never would.

Would killing this Mentor, the man who had done all this to me, the man I should hate and did hate most in the realms, bring me solace? Would revenge against him and the avenging of my parents be worth a hate-filled heart? Did it really matter, seeing that it could never bring my parents back? That it would change nothing?

These were stupid questions. The answer to all of them was obvious. So simple. For I already had a hate-filled heart. And I could not and should not bring myself ever to forgive such a man. Especially if he was after my friend, my sister. And if my maddened soul-sister was correct, then he was also after me.

I would kill him. And I would enjoy doing so.

Because, as much as I agreed with Treth that we hunted for love, I needed this.

The Mentor would die. By my hand. This year, next year, in ten or twenty years. It didn't matter. I had waited this long for my revenge. I could wait until eternity, as long as eternity ended with my blade through his heart.

***

"Why are you taking so long to choose? They're all swords!" Brett exclaimed, as we stood in the packed night market of Long Street, Old Town. We were surrounded by fellow shoppers, the warmth of golden streetlights and the smell of splendidly greasy street food. Brett was munching on some shrimp pad thai, using a plastic fork, while I was deftly handling my chopsticks on some chicken chow mein.

"That dire-rat horde netted us a decent wage," I replied. "I want to spend it on something worthy of the Crusaders."

"Kat's Crusaders," he corrected, pointing a shrimp at me.

"I'm not calling it that."

"I am."

"Good for you."

He grinned and ate the shrimp.

I wasn't just looking at any sword-stall like last year. This stall was run by a swordsmith from the Highland Kingdom. A quite renowned one. Last year, I had been more frugal, and would not have dared approach a stall of such a master smith. But now that I knew I was committed to this way of life, I felt I needed weapons worthy of my many challenges. And I was getting sick of Brett's clunky swords.

The Crusaders had been taking on a lot of jobs. The stuff that agencies didn't want. My old bread and butter. You'd think that meant we weren't making good money. You'd be wrong. Underneath all the high paying, big league jobs were a mountain of missions that needed solving. Too many for the agencies to handle. They were usually reserved for freelancers, like I had been. But, many of these missions weren't suited for single freelancers.

The Crusaders contained a Holy Light purifier, a demolitions and breaching expert, a machine-gun expert with extensive monster knowledge and a swordswoman with a ghost inside her head. That made us special. We weren't a big-name agency, but we weren't a lone freelancer either.

As a result, we had come to carve a niche for ourselves in the monster hunting industry, taking the jobs too small for agencies but too big for freelancers.

I was paying Cindy rent, I paid my old landlord the back-rent (despite Brett and Treth's reluctance), and we were churning a profit. Brett and Guy were beginning to regrow their sold and confiscated arsenal. I had bought new body-armour. And now, it was time to replace my swords.

I glanced over the prices of the enchanted swords, already prepared with hardening, purification and extra slice-ability. I winced and looked away. We were doing well, but not that well.

"Can I help you, miss?" a shop assistant said, standing on the other side of the plate-glass protected stall.

"Um…" I said, if that could really be considered *saying* something. "I'm looking for something battle-ready."

The shop-assistant smiled, that insincere retail smile.

"Certainly. Everything by Master Menzies is battle-ready. He caters to monster hunters, special forces, even the Thunder Corps."

"Interesting," Brett commented, while chewing. "Why is he selling his stuff on Long Street, then?"

"Brett…"

"No, miss, it's a valid question." The shop assistant looked pointedly at Brett. "Hope City has a thriving monster hunting industry, sir. Not just from the mega-agencies, but from every freelancer on the ground. Menzies Smithies makes as much money from selling at the night market as it does from special orders to Puretide."

"I hope that selling to freelancers means that there's some good deals for us small fries," I said.

"There is something for everyone. What type of monsters do you hunt?"

"Undead, mostly."

He almost frowned but caught himself. "A Menzies blade may not be necessary…"

"You ever faced down a zombie horde, bub?" Brett interrupted him.

"No, but…"

"Then," Brett turned to me, "we should explain what we're looking for. We might not make them, but we know about our weapons."

"Certainty, sir. Miss?"

Startled, and a little embarrassed by Brett's assertiveness, I took time to respond.

"I hunt more than just undead," I said. "So, I need something generalised. Fast enough that I can respond to attackers, but sturdy enough that it won't snap in combat. It will be cutting a lot of bone. Hand-protection and something to ensure the blade doesn't go flying out of my hand when I'm winded is also needed. Um…"

"Silver?" Brett offered.

I shook my head. "Silver dulls too quickly. I'll rely on your silver when we need it."

"If I may suggest something, if it is spirits or vampires you are hunting, a purification enchantment may do as well as silver. It won't apply to werewolves, however."

I nodded. It sounded good, but seeing the mark-up of their enchantments here, I may get whatever swords I bought enchanted somewhere else.

"So, anything that fits my description? Oh, and most importantly. I need two of them. I'm a dual-wielder."

The shop assistant contemplated my question, finally answering.

"There's one set in stock I think you'll like. Follow me, please."

He led us down the row of displays, until I saw the swords in question myself.

"Dual Menzies forged steel, of course. The hand-guard comes pre-prepared for enchanting prescriptions, so the blade can be customised as you wish. The cutlass style blade is fast and durable."

"A cutlass, Kat?" Brett grinned, joke incoming. "You should wear an eye-patch over your new eye so you can go full pirate."

"Hardy-har."

"It's aaaarrrr, actually."

The shop assistant didn't look amused.

"Can I try the grip?"

"Certainly."

He unlocked the display and reached for the swords. I saw the security guard standing behind him look over our way, in case we were inclined to make a run for it. He was carrying both a Menzies-smithed sword and a pistol. Luckily for us, we weren't the thief types.

The sword's weight felt good in my hand. Better than my dusack and wakizashi, in fact. I felt like I was suddenly betraying my old swords but examined the blades of these cutlasses more intently. They were about the same length as my old swords. Maybe half an inch longer. They had a nice curve to them, and the steel looked good. I passed the blade back.

"If you are still undecided, I can demonstrate its cutting power."

"Yes, please."

He took out a cylinder of ballistic gel, designed for demonstrating the power of any sort of kinetic weapon, and set it up on a hook hanging from the stall's make-shift roofing. Inside the confines of the stall, he didn't have to worry about hitting anyone around him.

He took a stance reminiscent of a fencer, pulled back the blade, and with a swift blow, severed the ballistic gel in two. At the consistency of human flesh, that was impressive. And the speed…

"I'll ta…" I stopped myself. *Haggle, Kat!* Don't look too eager.

"How much for the pair?"

"For you?" He considered a price. "$10 000."

I almost spat out my non-existent coffee.

"I could buy a .50 Cal Anti-Material Rifle for that price," Brett exclaimed. He was partly lying. He couldn't – legally. But that hadn't stopped him before.

"These are exclusive, Menzies designed and forged premium short hunting cutlasses, sir. That price comes with the territory."

"I've heard of high balling," I said. "But that price is ridiculous."

"Miss! You insult me. But I will go lower. How does $9000 sound?"

"Still, I could buy a lot of guns – which I insist are better than swords – for that amount."

"Miss?"

"Go lower."

"Miss, how about you name a price?"

"$2000."

"Miss! That is much too low."

"Meet me in the middle?"

"These are two of the finest swords you will see in Hope City. Nay! The world."

"And no freelancer will be able to afford them. They're good, I'll grant you that, but that price isn't worth it. And besides, you don't think I need them for zombie hunting."

"I didn't say that…"

"But you thought it. Fine, $3000."

He sighed. "The lowest I can go is $6000. And I'm only going that low because I need the sale for my daily quota.

Any lower and it won't count as a sale. Might as well pretend it was stolen and get the insurance."

"Well, we could help…"

The security guard grunted. No chance of that then.

$6000. We had been doing well. But not that well. Between the troll, dire-rats, a lot of zombies and a ghoul infestation, I had netted myself only $4000. And I needed some of it for food, rent and other things. I couldn't afford these swords. No matter how much I wanted them.

I prepared myself to turn them down, feeling Treth's disappointment as well. He had liked them too.

Brett touched my arm. Surprised, I looked at him.

"I'll pitch in."

"What? No…"

"Call it a business expense." He grinned.

"What about replacing your gear?"

"Guy and I have enough already. Cindy says we're hoarders."

"Well, she has a point."

"And you need a new pair of swords."

"But, Brett…"

"You can pay me back."

"Oh, if that's the case…"

"With a date."

"What?"

Before I could refuse or contemplate what was going on, Brett handed over his card to the assistant and sent over the money. While carrying the swords back home, I realised that Brett had paid the full amount.

Chapter 15. Demons

"Behind you!" I shouted. Cindy ducked just in time as the spectre loomed over her and let out a visible wail of dark energy, withering away even the dust in the air. She spun on her heels and released a blast of golden energy. Purification magic. One of Cindy's affinities as a sorceress. While she was an adept wizard, she was also a natural sorcerer, with a spark attuned to light magic. Unfortunately, her instinctive response didn't have much of an effect. The spectre flinched at the golden light and responded with a deafening screech.

Stunned, Cindy stared at the creature. I dive-tackled her out of the way as it swooped down on her. If it made contact with her flesh, then she may as well be the now withered dust.

"I thought it was a dark spirit," she exclaimed.

"Now that's just presumptuous!"

I helped her to her feet as the spectre considered us. It resembled an old man, translucent and floating off the ground. His mouth was elongated and twisted, and his eyes were angry.

"Its ethereal. We need to breach the In Between to put it down."

"And that's why Brett is taking so long?"

"8mm rounds are not common."

The spectre, impatient at our nattering, let out a challenging cry and soared across the room. I took a step back. Treth stopped me.

"Use the mirror across the room. It might have a silver backing."

Check that! Treth was wizening up about something other than the undead.

"Cindy, keep it busy!"

"How?"

Too late. I ducked at the last minute, sliding across the tiling and underneath the spirit. Cindy let out a blast of purification magic. More to stun it, as the magic couldn't pass through the In Between.

I trusted that Cindy would keep the spirit at bay and retrieved the large oval mirror. It had fancy ornate framing and a thick layer of dust on its front.

I lifted it off its wall-hanging and held it like a wide bat. It wouldn't be the first time I had used something really unsuitable for spirit hunting. In hindsight, we should have stocked up on ammo for Voidshot before we arrived. But the damn client told us it was a wraith. So, we thought Cindy's purification would suffice against the ostensibly and undeniably dark spirit. It wasn't a wraith, but rather, a more morally ambivalent spectre. Before we could fall back and go and retrieve the proper equipment, the spectre invaded a neighbour's house through the wall. Brett went to retrieve ammo while we kept it busy, allowing the homeowner to escape.

"I really hope this has silver," I grunted through gritted teeth. I held it up like a bat, ready to swing, and charged.

Cindy saw me approach, let out another blast of golden energy, and dove away from the spirit. It turned just as I belted it across its ethereal body with the mirror. I felt resistance and a surge of excitement. The mirror had silver! It could make contact. I heard a crash and saw the sprinkling of reflective glass cascade onto the ground.

Oops...

I hope the owner's lack of dusting of it meant it wasn't a beloved heirloom. Or perhaps the dust was an indicator of how old and beloved an heirloom it really was. Well, that was a discussion for after we got a spectre out of their house.

The spectre jolted at the sudden impact on its translucent back and turned to me, its eyes full of rage. If Cindy hadn't already tried purification magic on it, I'd have been convinced that it was a dark spirit. But you learn something new every day. Hopefully, in time for it to save your life.

The spectre inhaled, readying its deathly bellow, when it stopped at the sudden bang of Brett slamming the door inwards. I winced as I started tallying the increasing damages we would need to pay.

Brett levelled Voidshot at the spectre. It paused its inhaling and glanced at the silver Mauser. Before Brett could get a bead on it, it flew up towards the ceiling, and began whizzing around in a circle like a shark that had drunk too much coffee.

Brett fired two shots, putting even more collateral damage into the ceiling.

"Hold your fire! I'll get it," I yelled. Brett held, but maintained his aim.

"Get your timing right, Kat. I'd rather we don't wither away just yet," Treth commented.

Who did he take me for? Of course, I'd get my timing right!

I held the mirror like a bat again, levelled for a low-ball and aimed at the spectre on the roof. I traced its movements. And spotted a pattern.

I jumped, swinging the mirror above my head. It made contact! I felt the thud as the spectre was flung towards the ground by the force of my blow. Before it could recover, I pounced on top of it, pressing the mirror into it. It screeched, but the silver backing blocked the withering effect while also keeping it pinned.

"Take the shot!"

Brett fired, and I felt the vibrations and resistance below me subside. The mirror, with me on top of it, collapsed to the ground, causing increased shattering.

Satisfied, Brett holstered Voidshot and offered me a hand, that I accepted.

"I could have sworn it was a dark spirit," Cindy said, a bit shaken.

"You specialise in demons, Cindy. I thought it was dark before your purification didn't hit it."

"Well, you specialise in undead, yet…" Brett stopped as I glared at him. Cindy was undeniably more skilled than I in many respects, but I had had the benefit of a more diverse portfolio of monster kills. But I would almost kill for Cindy's ability to just shoo evil spirits and lesser demons away with her purification blasts!

"Here's your gun back," Brett said, passing me the holster and Voidshot, now disconnected from his belt.

I nodded my thanks and reattached it to my belt, hiding it below my back and behind my coat.

"What took you so long?" I asked.

"You do realise the closest gun shop that sells 8mm is in Old Town, right?"

I pretended to look stern but couldn't help but grin mischievously. Brett had actually made record time, all things considered.

The door opened, the creaking of its hinges sounding uneven. I really hope Brett didn't damage the door too badly.

"Wha…what happened?" the owner of the house asked.

"Spectre, madam," Cindy explained. "Evil spirit. We apologise and will recoup any damages. We were eliminating a haunting for your neighbour when the spirit escaped to your home."

"Ronald explained that," she said. "But…but…what did you do to my house?"

"The spirit wouldn't react to magic. So…"

"We had to improvise," I interjected.

"By destroying my great-grandmother's mirror?"

Oh, shit. Heirloom.

"Silver is one of the few things that can damage a spirit. We needed to weaken it so we could exorcise it with our apparatus," Cindy said.

"Wait…there's silver in the mirror?"

"Yes," I answered. "A lot of old mirrors have silver lining behind the glass."

The bemused horror on the woman's face turned to one of delight.

"That damn mirror has been sitting there collecting dust for ages! If it has silver, I can damn finally sell it for something. Thank you!"

Brett and I, seeing the opportunity to escape a pleased bystander before she found another reason to get angry with us, started sneaking away. Cindy, the paragon of virtue that she is, stayed put.

"Can you fill in your insurance details or payment details so we can compensate you for the collateral damage?"

The woman was muttering happily to herself as she investigated the mirror and confirmed that the backing was silver.

"Madam?"

She didn't respond.

"Come on, Cindy," I said, quietly.

Cindy frowned, checked her watch, and then followed us outside.

"How did Guy's hunt go?" I asked Brett, once we were outside.

"He isn't done. Probably having a blast."

I frowned. "Is he okay? Need reinforcements?"

"I don't think we'll be much help. He's hunting a bunch of ghouls in a warehouse with a flamethrower. I think if you can do it with swords, he can do it with a lot of fire. And besides – we don't want to ruin his fun. I don't think he's had his fill yet…"

Brett looked away and whispered under his breath. "Or ever will."

"Have you?" I asked.

"Of killing vampires?"

"Yes." I nodded.

His creased forehead made him look a lot older than his years and his contemplative frown made it obvious that he wasn't too sure himself. He didn't answer me.

"Anyway, folks," Cindy said, turning around and walking backwards. She looked to be in a hurry. "I have a staff meeting at the Memorial Children's hospital. I'll see you guys for drinks at 7?"

"Sure, Cindy. Have fun."

She smiled and waved us goodbye as she got into her car and drove away. Leaving me with Brett on a suburban street, slowly emptying of bystanders as they realised the hunt was over. We spotted our client, Ronald, just a bit away and approached him.

"Is the old man gone?"

"The spectre has been banished. You can confirm with your neighbour," I replied.

"And if he comes back?"

"If it is the same one, then you get a full refund and we'll come back to finish the job."

"If it is a different spectre," Brett added. "Your house is cursed. But we'll be more than happy to banish the next one."

He paused.

"For a fee."

I elbowed Brett lightly in the ribs. He grinned. He was being honest, though. Just – time and place.

Ronald sighed in relief. "I can finally sleep again. Thank you! I wire the money through MonsterSlayer? Right?"

"We prefer hard cash," Brett said. I elbowed him again. "If you don't mind."

"I don't," he answered, despite my display of minor abuse of my colleague.

He drew out a wallet and offered us a thick stack of bills. Brett counted it quickly, flipping through the notes like an experienced bazaar merchant. He nodded, satisfied, took a small amount of the bills and passed the rest to me. Because our agency was apparently called "Kat's Crusaders", I was in charge of distributing the cash. I'd split this lump sum with Cindy tonight.

We thanked Ronald and made our way down the street.

"Where did you park the van?" I asked.

"Traffic was backed up till Goldfield. Had to park a few blocks away." He answered.

"You ran a few blocks to get back to us?"

He shrugged. "We had to run longer distances and faster in the Corps."

I felt myself beginning to feel somewhat uncomfortable. I liked Brett. I really liked Brett. But reminding myself that he was a member of a then and now illegal death squad was…disconcerting. But he was my friend. And maybe…I don't know. Maybe, something more. I'd have to hear about it eventually. Would have to get over it. But before then, I needed to know what he did, and why.

"Brett," I said, quietly. The street was empty. Except for a pixie singing to some flowers. I wonder if Duer knew him? Actually, that's a bit racist. Not all pixies know each other!

"Yes?"

"What was it like?"

"What was what like?"

I hesitated. "The Corps."

He grimaced and I regretted the question. He must have seen my reaction and he put his hand on my shoulder.

"It's a long story, Kat. And I would like to tell you. Some of it. All of it. But in time."

"If you want to…"

He mulled over that statement for a while.

"I think I do."

He laughed, quietly, briefly, and without humour. I didn't like the sad look in his eyes.

"The Corps…was a lot of things. In practice, it wasn't so different from what we do now. Except…we weren't really doing it legally, so we had to dodge cops. Keep away from reporters. All that stuff. We had a government mandate, but we were deniable assets."

He looked down and his expression was the darkest I'd ever seen on him before.

"And that's how they could deny when half a hundred kids died in a town in the arse end of the void," he whispered.

"Did you really join them when you were a kid?"

"You started fighting monsters when you were a kid, Katty."

"I thought we agreed to stop that nickname. And I was 17. Not as young as you were. And I thought I was special."

He faintly smiled at the darkness of the humour.

"You're right. I started young. Too young. Didn't really have a fun adolescence. Well, some of it was fun, but that wasn't the point."

"What was the point?"

He stopped. I averted my gaze, embarrassed.

"Sorry…"

"The point? I think…"

He looked towards the sky and muttered something. I strained my ears and could make out "…the end of the world."

He looked at me suddenly, and I almost jumped.

"It was about revenge, initially. I had a vendetta. The Corps allowed me to fulfil it. And after that…I don't know. It all started blending into one. A single big blur of killing, hiding, exterminating, running, seeing friends die, seeing enemies die, slaying, dying…"

His eyes were glazed over, and his voice had sped up. He stopped suddenly. Lucidity returned to him. He begun walking again and I continued. A thought occurred to me, and it was something that could lead us off this disturbing topic.

"Brett...when you rammed those cops last year...what was going through your head?"

"That I hate cops."

"Seriously."

He sighed. "I...I don't know, Kat. When I saw them...when I got Conrad's warning...I just saw red. I tasted iron. And I felt like I was back in that blur. I didn't even know I had rammed them until I saw you face to face. Before then...it was like I was in the Corps again. A mindless killer. Good for a single thing..."

"You're not a mindless killer," I said, a little bit too loudly. A passing driver, his window open, stared at us, bemused.

"Then what am I?" he asked. His tone was...defeated.

I pushed in front of him and stopped, facing him and putting my hands on my hips. He was taller than me, despite my own respectable height, but I felt my presence made up for it.

"You're not a mindless killer," I repeated, in a quieter voice.

He looked down, and I saw him clench his fists.

"I spent the best years of my life killing, Kat," he started out sternly, and then mounted towards a yell. "Killing for the Corps. Killing for Drakenbane. And when I'm in the moment of killing, there is no remorse. There is no thought. I kill. And my mind has nothing to do with it. In that moment, I'm not Brett. I'm the slayer. I'm the hunter. And nothing else matters but the kill…"

His yelling boiled my blood and I considered yelling back. To duel his anger with my own, but I looked into his eyes. His sad eyes. Defeated. Lonely. He wasn't looking at me. He was looking at something long in his past.

My glare dissipated. And before I felt moisture in my eyes, I attacked him, embracing him with the tightest hug I could muster. It caught him by surprise, and I felt him take a step back before steadying.

"You're wrong, Brett. Because I know why you faced those cops. And I know why you helped me save Trudie. And I know why you keep doing this. But more than all that…I know why I want to spend time with you."

"I…I don't know, Kat." He didn't have a sob in his voice, but there was an undeniable despair.

"We all have our demons, Brett. And we can all fight them. And we can all try to save ourselves…and help others do the same."

I felt Treth watching us and anticipated his displeasure at my embracing of Brett. But I didn't feel anything like that. Treth was smiling, while tears ran down his face. My words meant something to him. Something deeper than I think I had already started, but that my male companions needed to embrace.

"I'm with you, Brett," I said, and sent an internal message to Treth. The message was also meant for him. "There's light beyond the darkness. And we'll find it together."

Chapter 16. Far from Home

Duer had been moping for the last few days, despite a generous influx of honey, vodka and English mustard (his new favourite dish). Both Cindy and I had been spoiling him, as we didn't coordinate on who shopped for him. As a result, Duer was doubly fed. Fae didn't exactly put on weight, but I did note that the scent of booze and sweets was heavier around him, and that his cheeks did seem a little rounder.

But, even with this pampering, he was still singing less, his glow was less splendid, and the flowers were not permanently in bloom as they were before, with his aid. In between hunts, I noticed his less than cheerful demeanour, and that even my cat was not trying to hunt him. Alex may be a predator, but fae were powerful beings. Even a hungry cat would take pity on one so crestfallen.

It was when Duer's glow was dimmer than that of an uncharged cell phone that I decided to talk to him. Cindy was out of the house – association meeting – and Brett was helping Guy with something that they insisted was too boring to even explain. That definitely piqued my interest, but Duer was what dominated my attention.

"Hey, bud," I greeted him, resting my elbows on the table-top next to his pot plants. "How're you doing?"

His glow twinkled briefly as I spoke, but soon faded to its depressed hue.

"Ye never call me bud," he said, sceptically.

I poked him, lightly. Instead of batting my finger away or threatening destruction upon my house, he just…well…let me.

"Duer…how long have we known each other?"

He looked at me askance, and then back at his wilting plants.

"Ye know that pixies don't keep time like you."

"Fifty-seven moons and thirty-eight jumps of the ram?"

He looked at my stupid grin with a look of both abject bemusement and horror.

"That's not even close!" At least he sounded a bit more energetic.

My grin faded and I leaned my head closer to him. I heard a faint purr as Alex saw my squatting down as invitation to wrap himself around my legs and nuzzle my knees.

"I know there's something bothering you, Duer. For the last while. And I want to know what it is."

"Ye got ye own troubles, Maddy." He waved my words away. A distinctly human gesture he had picked up from me, probably.

"In case you haven't noticed, my pixie companion, I'm doing pretty great. I've got a good team, enough money, a roof over my head, great new swords, and…"

I pictured Trudie and Pranish as I wanted to say friends. But it seemed I didn't have that anymore. And I didn't know if I'd get it back. Not with Trudie out there, practically Rifts away, and Pranish being his new bitter self. But that wasn't something I needed to lay down at Duer's tiny feet. He needed me right now.

"Duer," I said, much more quietly and sombrely. "Please tell me what's wrong. I want to help."

He stared morosely at his plant, not sparing me a glance.

"I'll give you some of that premium honey you like."

No response.

My frown must have been so deep it was etching marks into my face. I didn't know how to deal with a depressed pixie. Rifts! I didn't even know how to handle a depressed human. Do any of us?

I slowly stood up, to give Duer space, but as I turned my back, he spoke, coming out in his gentle lilt.

"It can't be helped. It's too late."

"What can't be helped?" I turned back to him, and he was looking right at me. I felt his gaze more intensely than almost any other gaze before. Even so his eyes were tiny, I could still make out the contents of his soul within. Duer was deeply broken.

I slowly leaned back towards him and offered him my hand. He stepped on and I stood up, watching my butterfly-winged friend sit down, holding his knees.

"I...Kat...I miss my family. I miss my kinth. I miss home."

"Oh, Duer..."

"And I know that I can't afford to miss it. That it isn't a pixie's place to yearn for what they can't have. And I tell myself, *Ye must move on.*"

He looked straight up at me.

"But I can't, Kat. I can't move on. Not while I know that I ain't gonna ever see my boy grow up. That I won't ever see me love again. And it hurts, Kat. It hurts more than I thought anything could hurt. And there comes times when I just want it to stop. To stop missing them. To stop remembering my kinth I left behind."

"Left behind?"

I had learnt what a kinth was from Duer. It wasn't his real family on his homeworld. A kinth was an adopted family, of sorts.

He sighed. "I told ye once that I'd tell you how I got my scar?"

"You said it would be a heroic tale." I tried to smile. Failed.

"It isn't," he said, bluntly. "And this scar ain't for me glory. It is my shame. For it meant failure for me. Failure for my kinth. And what could be eternity in the darkness."

"What…what happened?"

"When we came through the rift, we thought we had died. The creepers in the In Between had taken some of us already. We feared we were among the dead. Through the torrents of the void, we lost a lot of our already meagre equipment. When we landed on your world, we were broken."

He shook his head, as if trying to shake away the memories.

"We couldn't put up a fight. Giants. Filthy, bearded, wearing dirty brown jackets and carrying nets and traps descended on us."

Fae hunters – just thinking about them made me want to puke. I should have killed the fae hunter that tried to take Duer last year. Letting one of his ilk live in this world…it was like sparing a zombie.

"We fought. I fought. And I tried. I tried to keep us all together. But…"

A sob broke through his lips, and I couldn't help but cup my one hand over him, shielding him from nothing in particular, but it was something I felt I needed to do.

"Only some of us got out," he said. "Only four of the kinth. We found a place to sleep. We didn't know what it was. It looked like a cave. But I now know what it was. It was a drain. In the morning, stenching water pushed us out of our hiding place. Me wings were coated with dirt, but Brivvy managed to keep me in the air. Kat, can I have the honey now?"

"Yes, Duer. You can."

I carried him to the kitchen, where I opened the jar of honey and scooped out a teaspoon for him. He held it in both hands but didn't eat. He stared into the abyss.

"Eat, Duer. You don't need to tell me the rest."

"No…" he said, slowly. "I think I do."

Alex had jumped onto the counter, watching us with what I imagined was concern.

"The four of us looked for something familiar. Nature. We found a park. And while I can't feel the joy now, I remember feeling that we could live again. The green. The colours of the flowers. It was life. Not this artificial greyness. Not this lifeless rock. It wasn't like home, but it was the most like home we had ever found."

By the tone of his voice, I knew it didn't end like this.

"The giants came to us while we were asleep. I woke up as I heard Brivvy screech. He had her in his hands. She was trying to bite him, but he didn't care. His hide was too thick. I flew as fast as I could, beating at his hand so he would release Brivvy. But he didn't. No matter what I did…he didn't let go. The others tried to help. They flew around him, trying to distract him. Brivvy was still shouting. Shouting for me to take her spear. After I realised, I couldn't break his grip, I took her spear from her back, and I flew up his belly, dodging his hulking fists. I sped towards his forested face and looked him in the eye. I stabbed him. Triumph stunned me as he cried out, blood pouring from his eyeball. I didn't see his other hand come up, carrying a blade as large as me. Only luck that I didn't deserve pushed me backwards, so that only the tip brushed against my face. But the force brought blackness to me. When I awoke in the tall grass, they were all gone."

Gone. The word seemed to echo around the room, and in it I felt Duer's pent up emotions from possibly years of loneliness.

"Duer…" I said but struggled to find words. I looked at my tiny friend. My annoying roommate. My fae squatter. The little bastard. I loved him. He was a best friend. Someone I could come home to. A constant that I had started to take for granted. And he was hurting.

"Duer," I started again. "You're wrong."

He looked up at me, and I saw the faint trickle of tears on his face.

"You were heroic."

"But…Brivvy."

"Was probably saved by your sacrifice. You risked your life to save her. You faced down a giant…well, a human. That's pretty heroic sounding to me."

"But I lost them…"

"You fell into the tall grass, right? After being slashed?"

He nodded.

"Your kinth probably thought you were dead. And they needed to escape before they could find you. There's no guarantee that they're gone. As in dead, I mean. They could still be out there."

Duer mouthed the words, considering them. It was subtle, but a tinge of gold returned to his glow, and the pot plant didn't look as wilted anymore.

"My kinth…" he said. "Could still be out there."

I nodded. "Do you want to try find them?"

His glow faded. "I…I can't. It's impossible. A pixie is much too small for a world this big. I can't protect them from it. I can't even protect myself from it."

I felt a pang of empathy and sadness from Treth. He knew all too well how Duer was feeling. The two of them were very much alike, actually. Both outworlders, having to make the most of this new world. Both missing family. Both feeling they were to blame for things outside of their control.

"I would say it is impossible usually. But it just so happens that I have more favours to cash-in with a sleazy angel with lots of connections."

I let Duer gently down on the countertop, barely noting that Alex only sniffed him as he began licking the honey teaspoon.

I dialled Conrad.

"Kat of the legendary Kat's Crusaders? Phoning me? I'm honoured!" Conrad jibed over the phone.

"Hardy-har, Conrad. How're thing?"

"Cindy keeps me busy insisting that I write my memoirs. Yourself? Actually, you don't need to answer that. Kat's Crusaders is all over the hunter forums. Everybody is watching you."

"You don't seem the memoir writing type. But…" I glanced at Duer, who was gazing at me expectantly. "I need another last favour."

"I don't think you know what last means."

"I'm a drop-out. Bad at math. What do you expect? Anyway, you remember my pixie?"

"Dour?"

"Duer. Well, he has a kinth that he came through the rift with. A sort of adopted family of other pixies. But he was separated from them. We think that they may still be alive."

Conrad considered my words, and then spoke hushed, as if not wanting Duer to hear.

"Kat...pixies don't last long on Earth. You know that. If the fae hunters don't catch them and turn them into designer drugs, their antics tend to make them unwelcome in civilisation."

"Duer survived a long time on his own. And by the sound of it, his kinth was...is capable. I'm not asking for the world, but if you hear anything, could you let us know? His one kinth-mate's name was Brivvy."

"Pixie names don't come up in my usual gossip circles, Kat. But..." he sighed. "I'll do my best."

"Thanks, Conrad. You're an angel."

"I know...oh, and one other thing. I looked into Trudie's whereabouts..."

That shocked me. It wasn't like I had forgotten about Trudie, but the last few weeks of adrenaline and connecting with my hunter friends had distracted me.

"Your hacker friend was right. She didn't go to America. I found some footage of her boarding a bus to Goldfield. She looked dishevelled. Hair a mess. Not her usual self. No make-up. But it was her. I pulled a favour and got access to their ticket records. She bought it using her real name."

"Goldfield? Why Goldfield?"

"I came from Goldfield. Well, it was called Gauteng, then. It's big, Kat. The buildings are taller there. They make larger shadows. If you want to hide, then Goldfield is the place to do it. I daresay it makes our slums look quaint."

"Why is Trudie hiding?"

I felt his shrug through the phone. "That's your job to figure out. I'll see if I can find more details. I'll see you for drinks with the Crusaders next time."

"Definitely, Conrad. And thanks."

"Anytime, Kat."

He hung up and I immediately felt Duer's gaze. He was silently flying behind me, looming hopefully.

"He said he'll do his best," I answered.

"Do you think it's possible, Kat? That I'll see them again?"

Candace had asked a similar question before. I hadn't lied to her. And I wouldn't lie to Duer.

"I don't know, Duer. But I'll do whatever I can to make sure you do."

Chapter 17. Entrepreneurship

After blowing up a hundred-corpse monstrosity that had taken down squads of cops and Puretide operatives, this mission should've been a cakewalk. Why then was I lying on my back, out of breath, with my entire front covered with a black smear of necroblood where the abomination had hit me with a fist made of stomachs?

"Get around the side!" Brett yelled, yet his voice sounded fuzzy. Like I was listening to it through thick glass. I heard a ringing. Was my hearing protection not enough for all the gunfire? Or did I hit my head?

I felt a warmth come over me and saw a golden glow in my peripheral vision. My head cleared and I lifted myself up, with Cindy's help. She held a metal riot shield in one hand, protecting herself and her patient from shrapnel and splatter, as she used her free hand to heal and send purification blasts. After the quick healing spell, I felt as good as new. And she still looked like she could level a skyscraper with purification magic (assuming the skyscraper was essentially evil). If any of us got any serious injuries, however, she'd need to run the risk of tiring out her spark to heal us. She could possibly also use the local weyline, but that was a way slower approach. And this hulking undead monstrosity wasn't really giving us any time to rest.

I nodded my thanks to Cindy, who lifted her shield just in time as a chunk of black bloody flesh hit it, small bones clattering to the floor as the stickier bits of cadaver stuck to the surface and slowly dripped down like a slug on a window.

Brett had gotten off a point-blank blast with his shotgun, taking off a chunk of the abomination's leg. He retreated to a safe distance behind an overturned wooden table, manned by Guy, just before the abomination swiped at his previous position with a bloody, long arm, formed from the writhing flesh of the damned dead.

This abomination resembled some sort of troll-like humanoid. It was bulky, standing on two legs, with arms that almost touched the ground. It wasn't balanced, however. Candace briefly looked through my eyes and I felt her criticism for the undead creature. She had crafted a much larger beast last year. It had been a lot more lethal and a hell of a lot more effective at simply moving around. One of her less virtuous, if more impressive, feats.

This rift-borne abomination, by comparison, was clumsy, unable to guard itself from our many attacks. While

Candace's abomination had a rockhard hide, guarded by a sea of flailing arms, this abomination resembled a giant mutant zombie. Scary, yet inefficient. The otherworlder necromancer, who had created this beast that found itself stolen by a rift, lacked imagination. A skilled necromancer didn't try to imitate life. They took advantage of the privileges of undeath. Why make a giant rotting carcass when you could create a giant, walking tank made of flesh immune to bullets?

The human form was flawed. And it was the master necromancer's prerogative to fix those flaws.

While contemplating all this, I didn't know if these were my thoughts or Candace's. She was the necromancer, but I had been fighting undead for so long that I had begun to think a bit like them. Candace had told me that I would have made a powerful necromancer. Perhaps. But I didn't plan on finding out if there was any merit to her compliment. If I was to think like a necromancer, it would be all for the purpose of killing them and their minions. And if this Mentor, the man who had done all this to me, was as powerful as Candace made him out to be, I would need to understand all I could about his powers.

Brett peeked over his cover. The abomination still flailed, trying to balance on its now skeletal and shot gunned leg. Brett sprinted around the room, taking cover between the countertop of this old mess hall, and Cindy's shield.

"It's on its last leg." I couldn't see his grin through his mask, but I could hear it in his voice. "Here."

He passed me a cylinder with what must've been a fuse coming out of one end. A pipe-bomb. We didn't have the luxury of a mega-agency license to buy military-grade explosives, so we had to make do with some good old DIY.

"Roger," I replied. He took out his lighter. Always good to have a smoker in the group. Before lighting, he said,

"You've got about 15 seconds. If you can't get it in, then toss it as close as you can…"

I nodded.

"I'm serious, Kat. Don't be a hero."

"I'm always a hero." I stuck my tongue out, even though he wouldn't see it through my face-plate. Treth noticed and rolled his eyes.

Brett lit the pipe-bomb in my hand, and I bolted towards the monster. The abomination turned towards me, not caring for Guy's potshots anymore, and swung its bulbous fists in my direction.

I ducked underneath the rotting limb and slid across the floor, my coat shooting flames as if I was a race-car.

"Other fist," Treth said.

I ducked lower, rolled, and avoided an overhead swing from the other arm.

How many seconds left?

I hadn't been counting. But the fuse was getting short fast.

I bowled over onto my feet, instantly breaking into a sprint. This close to the beast, it couldn't attack me effectively. Like a basketball player going in for the winning dunk, I dropped the bomb into the creature's hollow torso, now drooping close enough to the floor after our wounding it.

Couldn't be long now.

In full sprint, I charged towards Guy's cover. He had already dropped his head. A split second after I vaulted over the table, I knew why. Flesh, blood, bone, and metal bits exploded outwards, piercing through the table and causing a few minor welts and bruises despite my now perturbed flaming coat trying its best to incinerate the projectiles.

I saw a trickle of blood as a piece of bone scraped through Guy's clothes and cut his arm. But he didn't seem to even notice.

A moment afterwards, it was over.

As was often the case after an earsplitting racket, the measured ambient sounds in the distance and the barely audible sounds of our own breathing seemed like silence. I breathed slowly. Once, twice. Bearings regained!

I stood up, feeling a slight ache in my knees and sides. The usual strain. Humans weren't meant to do what I do often. And I did it every second day! But despite the pain and exertion, I was loving it.

Brett stood up as I did. He took off his mask and was grinning from ear to ear. He held up his hand to high-five Cindy, who ignored him. I rolled my eyes and obliged him.

"Close call, there!" he said, loudly, his ears still adjusting to the now more reasonable volume.

"Pffft. Not at all. I had it in the bag."

A wince and hiss of pain caused me to turn to Guy, who was struggling to get up. Cindy rushed to him and started examining his limbs like a farrier would a horse. Her expression was impassive.

"It's just shrapnel." He tried to smile and winced instead.

"I'm going to do something for the pain and to stop infection," she said, like a professional doctor. "But we're gonna need to get those bones out before I apply proper healing."

Brett and I waited off to the side in a hall ravaged by black ooze and bone projectiles, as Cindy applied her golden light to Guy's wounds. I thought her manner initially cold. The way she usually acted while on the job. Cindy was warm sometimes, but there was an aloofness about her. As if she didn't want to be hurt, and that keeping people at a distance prevented her being hurt. But I saw something unique in the way Cindy applied her healing to Guy now. She was biting her lip. She never did that!

Curious.

Before I could ponder the thought any longer, or construct any gossip to discuss with Brett later, the front door to the building creaked open. A group of men wearing white combat gear entered. Their weapons were holstered or held at a relaxed stance, but there was an immediate hint of tension as they entered.

"I knew I smelled something bad!" the leader, a platinum blonde guy with a baby face, chided. "Necro-shit and a stepdown from that...the Crappy Crusaders."

"I know you didn't ever finish high school, Chet," Brett responded. "Doesn't mean you can pretend that you're still there."

Chet's face reddened.

"No need to get your pretty whites stained," I added. Shooing them away like one would an unwanted stray. "Puretide always arrives late. Good thing too. Means we can get dirty for you."

I grinned, toothily. "Also means we get paid."

The Puretide operatives looked everywhere but at us. Some of their faces were red. I noticed Hammond, standing aloof at the back with a cigarette in his mouth. He looked embarrassed. An odd look on the usually cocky as a cockatrice hunter. I also noticed that he stood apart from the main group. Like an outsider. I felt a stinging guilt that the reason for his aloofness was that he had no friends left after Garce manor.

Chet indicated Guy, who Cindy was helping up, looping his arm over her shoulders.

"Should get yourself some armour. Or is it…"

An operative put his hand on Chet's shoulder, stopping him. He shook his head and Chet looked disappointed.

"Let's go, guys. We've got proper bounties to collect."

They all exited the way they had come. All except for Hammond, who walked towards us, drawing a glance from one of the Puretide agents, but not much else. Hammond forced a grin.

"Charming gang," I said.

"He's right about one thing – you smell like shit."

"Cause we're rich as shit," Brett joked – badly.

Hammond looked down, taking a puff of his cigarette. He seemed to be examining the necro-blood splatter.

"I don't think Puretide could handle this."

He sounded sad. I put my hand on his armless shoulder. I had chopped off his arm last year to save him from a zombie infection. As a result, he seemed to think himself permanently in my debt.

"A pyromancer like you could've crisped this abomination up really good. Probably wouldn't even need improvised explosives."

He sighed.

"I know my spark is both boundless and beautiful, but this is some next-level stuff. Puretide has been declining. They're taking increasingly more niche cases."

He leaned in, whispering.

"We were paid to kill a dryad the other day. A fucking dryad! Collins refused. He got fired on the spot. I had the good fortune to have had a very convincing fake cough."

"Dryads are protected," Cindy said, carrying Guy and joining the circle.

"That's what Collins said. But, it's crazy. The brass isn't getting us to hunt undead or vamps no more. Like the Necrolord case took it out of them. There's no challenge anymore. Just reasonably paid jobs for almost no work. It's like we're ticks!"

"Hey, you could always join the Crusaders," I said, not really expecting him to accept.

He looked up, and his previously sombre expression immediately held an infectious grin. He turned to Brett and Guy.

"What do you guys think? Should I start working alongside this mad woman?"

Brett's face reddened.

"Kat's not mad!"

"I am, a bit."

"A pyro…" Guy panted through the pain. "Would be useful."

Cindy nodded her assent. We turned to Brett.

He crossed his arms and sighed.

"Yeah. I guess…if you want to."

Hammond beamed widely and offered his single hand. I shook it first. Then Guy, straining. And Cindy, also straining under Guy's weight. Brett considered it, and then shook.

"What's his problem?" Treth asked, looking askance at Brett, who was behaving like a teenager.

I had an idea. And it made me want to roll my eyes so hard that I may end up looking like a wight.

"I've got four more days on my contract, and then I'm a free man. Wait for me?"

I nodded.

"We'd keep a seat warm, but you can kinda do that yourself."

He turned his back to us and waved with his single hand, re-joining his soon to be not-comrades outside.

"Now," Cindy said. "Let's get you home and de-boned."

"Leave the ones I need, please," Guy answered.

"You talking about any in particular?" Brett grinned like a child. I elbowed him in the ribs.

He muttered. "Worth it."

***

"You sure about that Hammond guy?" Treth asked, when we were alone. Cindy was monitoring Guy at the clinic. Her surgery equipment was lacking the necessary apparatus. Brett had gone to get some new supplies to replace the explosives we had used. We had plenty of cash after that abomination, so shopping was a treat now rather than a painful necessity.

"I've saved his life and he's saved mine," I replied.

"What's your madness saying?" Duer asked. Oh yeah. Wasn't alone. But Duer didn't count.

"Ssshhh, Duer. I'm talking."

He rolled his eyes and then called Alex over to play with a piece of string.

"He reminds me of a rogue that joined my order," Treth said. "Got through two weeks of training before he was caught with half the silver."

"Weren't you a rogue before you joined the order?"

Treth blushed.

"You know?" I continued. "You're very much like Brett."

"How so?" he sounded affronted. "I'm not as childish as he is."

"You both don't like Hammond, for petty reasons. I'm pretty sure Brett doesn't like another male in the circle. Guy is fine cause they're practically brothers, but Hammond…he's competition."

"Competition for wha…oh…"

Treth emanated a profound discomfort. I laughed.

"It's pretty damn obvious that Brett likes me."

"And…do…you like him?" Treth asked, meekly. Much too meekly.

"You're sounding like a chastised schoolboy."

"I don't know what a chastised schoolboy is meant to be like."

I considered the question.

"I…like him. As a friend. As a colleague. If more…well, he's attractive."

"I'm sorry I asked."

"But you asked nonetheless."

I grinned but felt a tinge of sadness from my spiritual companion.

"Treth, I know you've had problems with Brett in the past, but through everything we've gone through with him, you should have gotten over that."

I frowned. "And it's not like I'm remotely interested in dating him…"

There was an unspoken, "Yet."

"Colin is…"

Treth nodded. He understood. But I still felt his melancholic mood.

"Treth," I asked, quietly. "Are you lonely?"

"Lonely?" he asked, trying to add some humour to his voice. He failed. "How can I be? It's crowded in here. I never get any peace."

"I know it's unfair…"

"That you have a body and I don't? That you can fall in love, but I shouldn't? Yeah…it is unfair."

"Treth…"

"No, Kat…it's fine. I'm sorry. It's not your fault. I know. But…but…"

"Treth, we'll find a way to get you a body."

That stopped him.

I smiled, weakly. "I've been making a lot of promises lately. Might as well add another."

"Are you sure, Kat?"

"You're right…it is getting crowded in here. And besides that, you should be allowed to be your own person."

"On Earth?"

"Where else?"

I felt both sadness and relief. A confusing combination. I guessed that Treth both missed Avathor, but also had reason to want to stay. Was that reason me?

"Kat…I loved Gorgo. You know that?"

"Yes, Treth. I do." Where did that come from, all of a sudden?

"And I still feel that I love her…but, I think I have moved on."

"Oh, Treth. That's good."

"Colin might not be here anymore, but you can fall in love again…"

I felt a sourness and melancholy come over me. Right now, thinking of dating someone other than Colin seemed impossible.

"I don't know, Treth."

"I do." His voice was intense. Confident. His intensity broke as I felt him grin.

"And if Brett is apparently like me, then he can't be all bad."

If Treth had ribs, I would have elbowed them.

Chapter 18. The Big Leagues

Guy had fully recovered within 24 hours. After the bone shrapnel and some large splinters had been removed, the wonders of magical medicine got him back on his feet and back in the fight. Even so, Cindy strong-armed him into taking a break, leaving some small odd jobs for Brett and myself to fill the Crusader's coffers. In the days that followed the abomination, Guy grew healthier and more and more bored. It was for this very reason that Guy was able to come barrelling into Cindy's lounge, as Brett and I were sharpening our blades, after dulling them on the hides of some undead goblin turtles (I was as surprised as you), and Cindy was reading a text that looked like it was written on a large dried fig leaf.

"What is it, Guy?" Brett asked. "Vampires in the well?"

Guy tried to speak immediately, but it was evident that he had been so excited that in his haste in coming to tell us, he had used up all of his breath.

"Hold up one finger if it is good news. Two if it's bad," Cindy offered.

He held up one finger. I felt a relief from a worry I didn't know I had. I was often a pessimist.

"Come on, then. Spit it out."

"Just…" he panted, then swallowed. He seemed to have re-gained his composure but was still buzzing with excitement. "I've just gotten off the phone with the head of security at Waterway Mall. A minotaur has burst through a rift. People panicking. It seems like it wants to make the mall into its new lair!"

"How is that good news?" I asked.

"We've been given prime mandate!"

That stunned me. Prime mandate meant we were not just first-come, first-served bounty hunters. We were the only ones allowed to collect at all.

"Why?" I asked, sceptically.

"The owner apparently has it out for Drakenbane after they overcharged him for a drake that they claimed was a wyvern. And Puretide isn't taking such large cases."

"Whiteshield?" I asked.

"Won't take it."

He wasn't just buzzing. He was practically quaking with excitement.

"We're the only ones who'll take it. But, that's if we take it now!"

Cindy put her leaf-parchment away and stood up, cricking her back. Brett did a final swipe of the whetstone on his machete and followed suit.

"What do we need for a minotaur?" I asked, sheathing my cutlasses and holstering Voidshot. My coat let out a small jet of flames. It was also excited. So was I.

"It's a man with a bullhead. I'm pretty sure that means it dies using whatever kills bulls and men," Brett said.

"That logic seldom applies," Cindy added.

Guy hastily indicated the door.

"Let's discuss this in the car. They've evacuated the mall, but our prime mandate may end the moment that the owner gets over his vendetta with Drakenbane."

"We've got 12 hours according to the law," Cindy said.

"But 12 hours is too long for people's lives and our rep," Guy replied. He turned his back on us and sprinted out the door.

"Packing pipe-bombs, shotgun and the sub," Brett said.

"Bringing the usual," I added.

"Brett, get a gun for me," Cindy added. That was unusual. She usually stayed out of the fight itself. Did she have experience with minotaurs?

She must have noticed my gaze, as she answered my unspoken question.

"Fought a cyclops once. They're both from the Olympian realm. They make monsters tough there."

She sighed.

"If only the bastard spawned tomorrow. A pyromancer would have helped a bunch. That bull hair must be pretty flammable."

We were a day off from Hammond joining the party. But a day was too long. We'd have to make do.

"We don't need fire slingers when we've got heated metal," Brett replied, carrying a backpack that felt like it weighed a tonne, with ease.

Guy hooted the van's horn, telling us to hurry up. Brett grinned.

"Let's not keep him waiting. We're in the big leagues now."

***

Guy violated as many traffic laws as he could reasonably get away with to get us to the mall. It was quite a distance away, nestled in between the Southern Suburbs (our home) and the Northern Suburbs (that mysterious land where people spoke with a slightly different accent). I'd been there a few times. It was more than a mall. It was practically its own little town. It was even walled in, keeping out monsters and policing itself with private security. What it lacked, however, were dedicated monster hunters. It thought that its high walls and generally well-armed security could deal with any random zombie that shambled in its direction. But rifts didn't care about walls. And it seemed that this minotaur didn't care too much about security guards.

On the way, almost jumping around the van as Guy went over curbs and jumped red lights, Cindy and I did a web search for the old Greek myths surrounding the minotaur.

"Says that Theseus killed the minotaur with a sword," I said aloud.

"Sounds right up your alley," Brett replied.

"It can't be that simple," Cindy added. "It never is with these Olympian machinations. The trickster gods of Olympus don't like doing anything straightforwardly."

"It seems that the catch was that Theseus needed to navigate the Labyrinth. He was given a roll of thread to find his way out."

"We don't need to do that," Guy replied, suddenly taking a sharp turn to avoid gridlocked traffic.

"When last did you go to Waterway?" Brett asked. "That place is a labyrinth!"

"A labyrinth for which we have a map," Cindy said, dryly. "No. I think it's more complicated than that. Minotaurs wouldn't be so much of a threat if their only difficulty was getting lost in a maze"

The top of a rollercoaster appeared in the distance. Waterways was attached to its own theme park. We were close.

"We go in a group, using security surveillance to track it down. I'm sure it is bestial, so we should be able to lure it out and outsmart it," Brett said, more professional and soldier like than before.

Cindy nodded. "We stick together. I don't want any casualties."

"There won't be any, Cin-cin," Brett chided. "You heard Hammond. We've got a mad cat on our side."

"I'm sure he said *mad woman*," I replied, rolling my eyes.

"I like this one better." He grinned.

"Deployment in five," Guy said. We took the signal and put our masks and helmets on.

We rounded the corner of the freeway and saw the looming gates of Waterway. Security was blocking people from entering. Guy scraped a few cars as he rushed past the parked bystanders. He only stopped as a security guard, carrying an SMG, stepped in the way. He screeched to a halt and held our newly printed agency IDs out towards the guard.

"Crusaders," he said, simply. The guard almost sighed in relief and indicated that we should pass. We heard shouts and crying from the crowd behind us. Relatives of those trapped within. I hoped we'd get to them in time.

I took a deep breath as we sped further towards the veritable labyrinth of Waterway Mall. I felt as if it would be a while before I could take another.

***

The usually bustling halls of Waterway were gloomy, quiet, ominous. A dark cloud had descended over the mega-mall, and the rift-surge must've knocked out the power. Maintenance staff were refusing to go inside to fix the power or kickstart the back-up generators while the beast was at large. That left us without the planned video surveillance. We would have to navigate like shoppers – using badly drawn maps and intuition. But it wasn't a case of finding the sports' store in this maze. It was about tracking a beast. And while there was no dirt to leave tracks, we followed another type of trail.

"I thought bulls were herbivores," Treth commented, morosely. "Yet so many people are missing chunks of flesh."

I could understand why the security had not re-entered the building, as we followed a stream of blood and death. Broken bodies of all demographics were like discarded ragdolls, across benches, bins, shattered pot plants and through the glass facades of shops. Some bodies were macabrely displayed next to collapsed mannequins, as if they had been bowling balls against pins. On closer inspection, my senses feeling every crunch of my feet on spilled glass and smelling every bit of iron in the air, I saw that the bodies were not stabbed or slashed. They had died on impact, thrown or bludgeoned by their killer.

I had faced massive monsters before. Even the troll had not been my largest foe. That honour went to Candace's monstrosity, which she had created when the darkness was at its strongest in her mind. But there was something else about this hunt. Something odd. Traversing these halls and the destruction that the monster had left in its wake, I could feel a collective unease descend upon us. It was not like we were predators tracking our prey in a wilderness. It felt as if we had entered the cave of a bear and there was no way out.

We had entered what must've been only minutes before, but already I was forgetting the way out. The path behind me was dark inside my mind. Was this an effect of the minotaur's dominion?

What else could it do?

I wished someone would speak, but all I had was the occasional comment by Treth, to whom I could not respond lest my reputation of being *mad* became literal.

I felt a hand on my shoulder as Brett indicated for us to keep moving. I tore my gaze away from the broken body of a girl who could have been my age. I pictured Trudie's form, like a shrivelled insect. I turned back to the Crusaders and kept moving. I wouldn't let this creature get away with it. No more death. Not if we could help it.

"Ancestors…" Guy whispered, under his breath. I echoed his sentiments. Turning into an atrium of the mall, dripping blood to the bottom floor in steady rivulets, were bodies, impaled on the metal posts that would have held now destroyed glass panes. The corpses' faces were stuck in eternal screams. Never ending pain and fear.

"There's darkness here," Cindy said, her eyes closed.

"No shit," Brett said, but even his voice was shaky.

"She means of the magical variety," I replied.

Cindy nodded. "There's a form of corruption emanating from those impaled…people."

"So…we're facing a minotaur wizard?" Brett asked.

"Perhaps. Kat, do you have demanzite?"

I nodded. Brett and Guy both indicated they were also holding onto the magic-cancelling powder. Cindy couldn't carry it herself. She had spark and coming into contact with the powder would cause her to become violently ill, catatonic and semi-paralysed for a long while.

"If it incants or casts anything, make sure to use it. Corruption magic is powerful. But my gut tells me that this thing isn't a wizard. This feels like a different form of magic. Not words of power, but a different type of language. As if communicating through the In Between with carnage and the natural language of gruesome death and malice."

"Can we do anything?" Guy asked.

"I wasn't expecting any sort of advanced dark magics, but we can try to break up the ritual. Removing the corpses from their impalement may work. But I suspect that the beast has made similar scenes throughout the mall."

"Every bit must count," I said. "Let's go up and see what we can do."

They nodded and we rounded the atrium, past the non-functioning elevators and towards the motionless but still usable escalators. Brett and Guy took point up either escalator. Cindy and I watched our backs. Besides the chaos and death, there was no evidence of a minotaur. We couldn't even hear so much as a footstep in the distance.

The impaled corpses were even more gruesome close up. We took turns standing guard and hoisting the corpses off their unseemly perches. We laid them down next to the poles. Once we were done, they could be claimed by their loved ones. For all the good that would do.

"Less dark, now," Cindy said, once we were done. "But I'm sensing a stream of corruption coming from below."

Her eyes widened.

"It's close. Moving...stopped."

She looked at us, shocked. "It's gone."

"Gone?"

She nodded, almost reluctantly. Like she didn't believe it herself.

"Are you sure?" I asked, my voice quiet as I anticipated a primal roar to bellow at any moment.

"I...don't know. I felt a strong presence on the floor below. A moving blob of corrupt energy. And then it just...vanished."

"It's a lead," Brett said. "Might as well follow it."

"Those who chase danger often find it," Treth recited, probably quoting his long dead master.

"Chasing danger is our profession," I said aloud, to answer Treth. The others nodded their agreement but did so with a sense of morbidity.

We climbed down the escalators again, going back into a darker patch of the mall as natural light couldn't penetrate the layers of shop-filled floors. Cindy led us further into the dark as we chased her hunch.

A crunch of glass. We all stopped, levelling weapons and spells all around us. My heart sped up. It didn't help that through the faded dark I could see more destruction and the bodies of hapless victims strewn over countertops, skewered by hockey sticks and missing their limbs.

It was darkest here and we had to turn on our flashlights. My coat acted like a beacon for the rest of the party. It thrummed in anticipation. It probably enjoyed the hunt more than I did. At least someone was enjoying this. I wondered if the salamander enjoyed being my coat.

"In there…" Cindy whispered, pointing towards a hardware store. Its usually blinking sensors were dark and two were knocked over, spewing wires and circuitry underneath their bases. There were some discarded shopping bags and spent 9mm shells on the ground. A security guard, missing the better part of his chest, was curled up in a ball near his 9mm pistol. Brett leant down to pick up the firearm, still training his shotgun into the darkness of the hardware store. We couldn't tell if the bullets had been at all effective. All the blood was indistinguishable. But it was telling that we did not see any minotaur corpses.

I swallowed down my trepidation and led the way into the darkness.

Counters had been abandoned, with goods still halfway through checkout. I saw tools, nails and all sorts of widgets strewn wherever our lights pooled. If we were inclined, we could have picked up some much-needed DIY supplies. One such thing we needed was duct tape. I stopped and crouched down to pick up a roll on the ground. Trudie always said that you could never have enough duct tape. And it wasn't stealing. I'd pay when this was all over.

A rattle and clatter caused us all to almost jump and point our flashlights towards the source of the noise.

A white and red figure darted further into the darkness. Through the silence, I heard a faint sob. Was it a survivor?

We converged on the location of the figure, too small to be the beast. Rapid footsteps and panting became louder as we approached. Finally, they stopped. We shone our lights at a young woman, covering her eyes from the light, and tears streaming down her face onto her bloodstained white shirt.

"We're here to help," Cindy said, breaking formation and approaching the woman.

"No, no!" the woman almost cried, but her voice was hoarse and quiet. She tried to fight Cindy, slapping and shoving, but the healer coerced her way through, and forced the woman's face onto her shoulder. I saw a faint glow as Cindy eased whatever pain she was going through. The sobs did not stop, but the woman's breathing calmed.

Cindy released the woman and let her collapse to her knees. We slowly approached her.

"What happened?" Cindy asked.

"Everyone…" she muttered, staring off into nothing. "Everyone is dead."

"Were you with anyone?"

"All dead."

Cindy frowned. I could see that she hated this. She didn't like to see people suffer. More so than any other decent person, even.

"Have you seen the monster?" Brett asked.

"Mo…monster? It…it…"

She covered her face, paling. Two sobs, and then she heaved, vomiting onto the ground.

Cindy put her hand on the woman's back.

Tenderly, she said. "We want to stop it. Please tell us what you can."

"It…it all went black. We couldn't see. I couldn't see. We only heard it. It sounded like a large animal. Then I couldn't hear it. Only the screams. And…" She sobbed, choking down on her words. "…bones breaking.

Crunching. Oh, Rifts! Where are they? They can't be…they just can't!"

Her weeping renewed as she covered her tear, spittle and vomit covered face with her hands.

Cindy stood up and looked at us earnestly. "We must help her get out."

"We're on a hunt," Brett said.

"And that's why we need to get her out of here. We can't leave her alone while that *thing* is roaming about."

Brett didn't argue. He knew better than to argue with Cindy. And I suspect that, despite his callous training, he did care about this unnamed woman, crying out for the, most likely, dead.

Cindy helped the woman to her feet.

"We're getting you out of here."

The woman didn't respond but didn't resist as Cindy pulled her along.

"The crusade is about saving," Treth said. "This is the right thing to do."

I didn't know if he was trying to convince me. I already agreed with him and Cindy. And I'm sure that Guy and Brett did too, at least a little bit.

Finding our way out of the dark store was easier than navigating within. There was a faint glow of natural light coming from the exit, and we followed it. There was, however, the problem of our faded memory of how to get out.

"We should have used thread," Brett muttered.

Guy stopped ahead of us, lowering his gun, as he found a map-board display. He traced his finger across the board, planning our route. I anticipated that we'd soon forget it and get lost again. Hopefully we would find another map before we got too lost. That, or we found the minotaur.

Or it found us.

The walk past abandoned stores and down the wide hall was a quiet one, with only the faint weeping of the woman and our footsteps to fill the silence. We were approaching natural light and could safely see without our flashlights. I almost breathed a sigh of relief when we made it back to the atrium area. At least we hadn't been turned around completely.

My relief was short-lived, as I heard a gasp of horror, and the woman pulled herself away from Cindy's reassuring grasp and bolted forward, howling like a banshee. She bolted to a man that could have been her age or much older. His lacerations and wounds made it hard to tell.

It seemed her first suspicion had been correct. They were all dead.

"Kat…"

Treth's warning was unneeded. The thumps, like a jackhammer, were warning enough.

The woman was halfway to her target when a gargantuan creature reared its misshapen head and charged towards her. I tried to cry out, but my words were silent beneath the rumbling of the minotaur's hooves.

Brett burst forward in front of me and barrelled towards the woman, who had become frozen in fear as she realised what was happening.

Her head almost whiplashed as Brett knocked her forward. The minotaur skidded to a halt, sliding on the tiles and barrelling into a donut kiosk, sending baked goods flying. Guy dove for cover behind a café table and opened fire on the creature. I didn't see any blood or impacts on the beast's flesh.

I spared Brett a glance. He was lifting himself up as the woman started crawling away. By Athena, she was going to get herself and all of us killed!

Despite the volleys of Guy's shots, the minotaur rose up over the annihilated kiosk, and stood its full height, bullets harmlessly pelting against its bare chest.

The creature was easily over 8 foot tall. Its pair of black, slightly curved horns put it at around 9. Its bull head did not look like any sort of bull I had seen before. Its head and upper torso were covered in thick, matted brown fur, but its almost bovine maw was lined with teeth that looked more at home in the mouth of a lion. It seemed that minotaur's didn't share cattle's dietary habits. Below this furry head was a still hairy, but not as furry, humanoid body, rippling with muscles and pulsating veins, with large human-looking hands, and cloven feet. It wore a loin cloth of pale brown. I was thankful for that, if anything. Around its neck was a necklace made of lumps of flesh, hooked onto a chain.

The minotaur let out a ground shaking roar as Cindy also opened fire on it. It charged towards me.

I dove out of the way, attempting to slash it as it passed. My coat flared up into a pillar of flame at the beast's approach. My blade whistled as it cut through the air, not meeting any resistance. The minotaur, running on all fours, had turned at the last second, making a beeline right for Brett and the woman.

"Brett!" Guy shouted. He kicked Brett's dropped shotgun across the tiles.

Cindy let out a flash of golden light that didn't seem to even slightly perturb the beast. Brett thought fast, kicking the woman out of the minotaur's way, and rolling himself. The minotaur stopped just short of running off the ledge and into the lower floor of the atrium. Brett caught the shotgun and lifted it. The minotaur loomed above him, standing on its hind legs. Smoke poured out of its fist sized nostrils. Brett fired and the minotaur flinched. Only slightly. It brought up a fist that could have doubled as a battering ram.

My sword sank into its ankle. But, rather than cry out in pain, it only grunted, and looked at me. Brett used the opportunity to get to his feet and fire a close-range shot into the creature's face.

"Kat, the cut…" Treth cried.

The wound which I'd made in the minotaur's ankle had already stitched up. As if I hadn't cut it in the first place. So, bullets couldn't penetrate it and it healed from blade wounds. What could kill this thing?

"Get away!" Cindy cried, releasing a bolt of honey-gold energy that pelted at the minotaur. Her voice was dripping with desperation that could even be heard over the crackle of her purification bolts.

The beast buckled as the blow hit it, but it regained its balance quickly, shoving its one hoof into the tiling, forming a crack in the floor. Brett and I took the chance to back away, still facing it. Its head spun, turning towards Cindy. It let out a cross between a roar and a demonic moo. The sound sent my stomach into revolt and I unconsciously backed away even more, all the while wanting to bring up the contents of my belly.

Guy fumbled as he reloaded his magazine, for all the good it would do him. Cindy was gesturing wildly while incanting. Her hair clung to her forehead.

In the past, the only one to be foolhardy had been me. It had been easy to be foolish then. Only I (and Treth) was putting my head on the chopping block. But here…we were all going to die.

That thought struck me like a tonne of bricks. Or more appropriately, like the minotaur's monstrous balled fist. My heart began racing and my pupils dilated. Treth sensed my panic rising.

"Run!" he yelled, breaking me from my stupor. I opened my mouth to repeat the order. Brett was side-stepping the downward blows from the invulnerable beast, while Cindy was incanting hard. We needed to get out of here. Her spark was needed for healing – not senseless and impotent attacks.

"Run!" I managed to yell. Brett froze at the command, for a split second, and time seemed to slow as the minotaur's massive hand swiped him from the side, sending him reeling into the atrium. Like a ragdoll, he went sailing over the edge. I couldn't hear him cry out. I could only hear my own scream, as I ran towards the edge myself. Treth and Cindy yelled for me to stop, but I couldn't. I dove over the edge, and into the blackness.

I hit the floor below with an oomph and felt shattered glass press through the gaps in my leg padding and into my flesh. My knees rang out like an overused church bell. And I heard distant gunfire from above.

"Brett!" I called, using my cutlasses to pull myself up.

I heard a muffled murmur in response. I couldn't see where from. The darkness was moving in closer. Ever closer. And as my heart beat faster and faster, I felt Candace watch me and begin to panic herself.

"Don't die, Kat! I can't bring you back."

I gritted my teeth and stepped forward. A pain shot through my legs and I fell again. More glass penetrated through my pants. The pain was a spread out but relatively mild burn across my skin. I didn't care. All that mattered was navigating this darkness. This unnatural labyrinth.

I had to find Brett.

I couldn't die. Not yet. Not if it meant he'd die too.

"K…k…kat?" I heard, barely a whisper.

"I'm coming, Brett! Just keep talking."

He coughed. It didn't sound good. I pulled myself up, scraping my blades across the ground. They suddenly felt too heavy. The gunfire had stopped upstairs. Oh, gods and rifts…not that…

"Get…" he coughed again. "Get outta here, Kat."

"Not without you!"

How much were we being paid for this? Was any amount worth this? Was any amount worth putting my life on the line? Worth putting Brett's life on the line?

I lurched forward. Step by step. Dragged down by shattered glass and the excessive quantity of blood. I used my blades to pull me forward, stabbing the ground as if they were ski poles. My vision blurred and I could only see for a few metres ahead of me.

"Brett…" I murmured, my voice growing hoarse.

"I…I'm here," he said, hushed, sounding groggy.

I turned my head and saw him, huddled on the floor, holding his side. I saw blood covering his hand, and a growing dark patch on his jacket. If I hadn't had a sword in both my hands, I would have covered my mouth.

This couldn't be happening. Not Brett. Not like this. I remembered what Treth had said last year. Brett would hurt me, he said. Hurt me like this. Hurt me because he was like me. And he could be taken away.

"I won't let you die!" I half sobbed, half yelled. I sheathed my swords and leant over him. He was pale, and while he tried to look at me, his eyes couldn't focus. As if he was looking at someone else, a thousand years ago and a thousand miles away. More blood was pooling around his wound. I put both my hands over it and tried to recall all the rudimentary medical training I had ever received.

242

Unfortunately, it amounted to passing tips that all disappeared out of my mind the moment I needed them.

"Kat…" he whispered. "Is that you?"

"Yes, Brett. It's me. You're going to be okay."

As if fate wanted to prove me wrong, the building vibrated as the sound of what could only be a tank falling from orbit boomed from nearby. I didn't want to turn around to see what it was. I knew it already.

"Kat…please go…"

"Shut up, Brett." I pressed his hand closer into his wound, and touched his forehead, smearing blood on his whitening skin.

Treth was apprehensive. He was looking behind us. And he was watching it move closer, its hooves thudding like the booming of artillery.

I clenched my fists as I looked at Brett's paling form. It couldn't end like this. I wouldn't let it end like this!

I stood up, ignoring the agony in my legs and the silence above. There was only my heartbeat, the thuds of cloven feet, and the deep inhalations of the towering beast before me, its red eyes glowing in the dark and its nasal steam both audible and viewable even at this distance.

I unsheathed my blade with a hiss but, as my other hand brushed past my pocket, I felt a lump. Two lumps. Treth sensed my epiphany, but he didn't know what I had planned. And I didn't know if it would even work. And even if it did, I doubted it would last long. But perhaps, long enough.

"Come and get me, shithead," I whispered, but recognition flickered in the red eye. Who knew a minotaur would be offended so easily?

I steeled myself for the pain in my legs and sprinted away from Brett. The minotaur bellowed its sick roar and tore after me, breaking tiles with its hooves.

I had to be quick. Very quick. Could my legs handle it?

I ran through the dark, sheathing my one cutlass and drawing out the pipe-bomb and duct tape. Sensing my anticipation, my coat flared, raising my field of vision. I stuck the pipe-bomb to the extended duct tape as I ran, holding both in one hand and pumping with the other. Through the dark and orange haze of my coat, I saw a bench and leapt onto it. I spun in mid-air. The minotaur was almost on top of me, charging full blast on all-fours. Time froze. Went slow-mo. And I calculated what I would need to do. A moment. Another. And it was under me. I twisted my torso and reached out with my free hand, catching its horn. Time sped up and my grip almost slipped. This was harder than any rodeo. Well, I imagined so. I'd never been in a rodeo. But a minotaur, charging through the unnatural darkness in a slaughterhouse of a mall must be more intense. I pulled my other arm up, attempting to attach it to the beast's horn. It bucked and I almost dropped the bomb. The smell also didn't help. It smelled like burnt animal hair and death. And the burning smell was understandable. This thing felt like an oven!

The minotaur turned suddenly, rushing back towards Brett. I needed to do this fast! Gathering all my strength, I managed to pull myself up onto the minotaur's back and gained a tighter grip on its ragged horn.

We were getting closer.

I hefted the roll of duct tape over the horn and started looping the attached pipe-bomb with more tape, until it was secure.

"Do it, Kat!" Treth encouraged me.

At least he believed in me. I'm not sure I did.

I had no lighter, but my coat obliged. It flared, scorching the minotaur's fur, but also lighting the fuse. I let go of the horn and kicked off, landing with a thud and colliding into a display.

Three.

Two.

One.

Boom.

The minotaur didn't stop even after the deafening blow, and my heart sank into my stomach.

"Kat, watch…"

It started swaying, hitting into stores on either side of the hall. It face-planted into the tiles, and skidded for a few more centimetres, until coming to a stop.

My body almost relaxed as the beast stopped moving but, remembering Brett sent my adrenaline spiking once again. I bolted towards him and found him still curled up. There was more and more blood.

I collapsed to my knees. His eyes were closed.

No…No…

I realised I had been saying it out loud.

"Kat, calm down," Treth said. "He's still breathing."

My eyes widened and I brought my ear to Brett's chest. There was a rasp to it, but he was definitely breathing.

"I'm getting you out of here, Brett."

"You need to stop the bleeding. Check his bag."

I lifted Brett up just enough to put my hand into his back-pack and fish out his first aid kit. I didn't know what I was meant to do. Everything was a blur.

"Pull up his shirt. Put that dressing over the wound," Treth said, speaking hurriedly but calmly.

I pulled up his shirt and almost bit my tongue. Brett's abdomen had a dark red slit in it worse than any knife, and it was cascading bloody ooze.

"Apply the dressing."

I pulled out a wad of what looked like white cloth and pressed it into the wound, tightly. The white started to take on red.

"Keep it hard. Need to stop the bleeding. Now, stick it down with that tape."

With my free hand, I retrieved the medical tape and used it to stick the dressing down tightly, finally biting it off with my teeth. I felt Brett's body vibrate slightly under my touch. At least it was still moving. But his breathing was getting more and more ragged.

"What else do I do, Treth?"

He didn't answer.

"What do I do?"

"Kat…" I understood by the tone of his voice what it was and turned my head.

The minotaur towered around ten metres away, holding itself steady on the corner of a jewellery store's façade. Its face bore hairless, red patches, oozing out bits of metal and rapidly re-growing fur.

"Why can't you just fucking die?"

I should have felt frightened. I should have felt despair. But with Brett lying comatose, and Treth speechless, I felt only a desperate rage come over me.

I stood up, completely ignoring the searing pains across my body. I drew both my swords with a simultaneous whistle-hiss of metal as I cut the air.

The minotaur grunted and stood tall, taking a step before me.

"I won't fucking move, you monster."

It cricked its too human and too large fists in response and took another step.

"You want to kill him? You'll have to kill me. And be warned. No one has managed to do that yet."

It started jogging towards me, its hooves breaking the tiles once more. I held my swords against my sides, like a fallen angel, and considered the beast. Its writhing, furred flesh. Its corruptive taint. And what it had done…

And what it would do…

And what I would stop.

"Hold the line, Kat. That's all we can do," Treth said.

And it was all I would need to do. With my friend behind me, bleeding out.

The minotaur broke into a run, rearing its horns at me. I held my swords before me. And closed my eyes.

I pictured Brett. I pictured Treth. I pictured my blades, glistening steel and blood. And a golden light, finding its way outside of my heart and into my blades.

I yelled. A voiceless, booming and incomprehensible cry, as I drove my twin blades into the minotaur's head. I expected resistance but felt none as my blades bit deep, sinking further and further, until I saw their points glisten with blood and steel through the other side of the beast's head. My body had not moved an inch backwards. I held the line.

I let go of the blades and felt a profound relief as the minotaur's body hit the ground with a thud that propelled shattered tiling into the air.

Like a tidal wave, everything hit me. The blood loss, the exhaustion, the trauma. I only managed to limp towards Brett's body, to confirm that he was still okay, as I collapsed and darkness claimed me.

Chapter 19. Perspective

It was usually me lying in the hospital bed. Alone with my fevered thoughts. Only the constancy of Treth's presence to keep me company in my dreamless, thoughtless state. I was used to being swaddled by the white sheets, waking up to the beeps of the heart monitor, and feeling the dull aches of the injuries that had failed to kill me.

I was not used to standing next to the bed. It was an odd experience for me, being completely lucid in this room, and to be the one looking down on Brett, as he breathed slowly, his eyes closed. How often had I put others through this experience? How often had Trudie and Pranish sat or stood by my side, watching the slow inflation and deflation of my chest, not knowing when it would stop? How often had they watched my heart monitor, guided only by scenes in movies to know if I was healthy or not? I knew now that the medical staff were not helpful. They didn't answer my questions. They just smiled, weakly, and rushed off to another patient. Most of them had sunken eyes. Like they had been physically drained of all their vitality. Well, of course they had! The sorcerers were channelling their spark directly into the patients while the wizards were playing with the primal words of power. I was present at Brett's surgery and watched Cindy, among other healers, remove a broken shard of minotaur claw and countless shards of glass from his rapidly deteriorating body. My rudimentary first aid, guided by Treth, had given him seconds. Only seconds. Cindy tried to tell me that those seconds possibly saved his life, but that wasn't it. If I had only done more, then Brett wouldn't be lying here right now. He'd be grinning that stupid smirk of his, calling me Katty, and insisting that we go shopping for ammunition and cola.

Tears welled up. I let them. There was only me in the dimly lit hospital room. Me, and Brett. And Treth, but I'm not sure if he counts. And Candace, kinda, but she was busy. Doing something. I hope nothing too dark. I hoped that our eyes still being exchanged would keep her from devolving back to her old ways.

With moist eyes, I touched Brett's hand. No response. Not even a twitch.

"You idiot," I murmured. "You fucking idiot."

I didn't know if I was talking about him or me. My legs still throbbed. They had been healed already, but there were always after effects. Always scars. I sat down, rubbing my knees.

Guy and Cindy had managed to get away from the minotaur, but they had not realised it would choose the easier prey and leap down to us. After they heard the boom as it impacted on the same floor as Brett and me, they did all they could to get to us. But from what Cindy learnt afterwards, the minotaur had actually turned the mall into its own labyrinth. Not physically, of course. But it didn't need to. Its corruption magic had twisted the perceptions of anyone else treading in its domain. We could have been in an empty hall and still got lost! But after the minotaur was killed, his hold over the mall dissipated. Guy and Cindy were able to find us quickly after that.

Cindy said that I had killed the minotaur. I vaguely remembered stabbing it. But how could that work when nothing else did? Bullets, bombs, and my slashes earlier did nothing. What did I do differently?

"You fulfilled the myth," Cindy suggested. "That's all I can think of. You did something that triggered the minotaur's weakness. Do you remember what you did?"

I couldn't answer her. I shook my head. All I had done was stab it. And somehow, my blades pierced its hide. I didn't think they would, but it was all I could do. All I could do to protect Brett behind me. And even then, he was still not okay. The doctors and healers told me he would be fine, but I didn't…couldn't believe them. But I had to. This was Brett! He'd shoved a grenade down a vampire's throat, traversed the entire city to find me when I was missing, and helped me wrestle down a troll. He would be okay. He had to be.

Because a large part of me couldn't think about what I would do if he wasn't.

"Get something to eat," Treth whispered. "He's not going anywhere."

"Not hungry," I answered, simply.

I sensed that Treth didn't believe me. But he didn't argue. What did he think of this? Did he feel vindicated? That Brett almost died? That his theory that Brett would not be a safe companion because he was also a hunter was at least partly true? No…I don't think so. Treth was too righteous for those sorts of thoughts. But he had predicted this.

But, then again, Colin hadn't been a hunter. Perhaps, everyone around me was doomed.

"Everything was going so well," I murmured. "But life just seems like its waiting for the next bad thing to happen.

If it wasn't this…then it could have been Cindy, or Guy, or me."

All three of those things somehow didn't seem as bad. And realising that made me feel not only a bit guilty, but also highly confused.

Who was Brett to me?

A friend?

A colleague?

A fellow hunter?

More?

I knew what I was thinking, but I couldn't vocalise it. Because, perhaps…I was afraid. And this event didn't help. For it reminded me…

That I could lose someone again. That I could have someone to lose.

Brett could be Colin. But Colin was dead. And Brett could die too.

And could I really go through that again?

"I don't think I can do it, Treth."

"I don't know what *it* is, Kat. But if you can't do it, nobody can."

I let out a short, quasi-amused snort, that held no mirth.

"Remember what the archdemon said? That I have a broken soul."

"I think he changed his mind on that."

"Broken or not…I feel stretched. Wrung out like a washcloth that has been handed down for a hundred years."

"We're still young, Kat."

"Yet…I feel so old. So jaded…"

I looked at Brett's comatose form.

"How does he do it, Treth? How does he smile despite everything that's happened to him? How does he make me smile despite everything that's happened to me?"

Treth was silent, for a long time. I reached out my hand again to touch Brett's and rub his knuckle with my thumb. His hand was warm. That had to be good, right?

"You love him," Treth said. It sounded, resigned. Before I could confirm or deny the claim, Brett's hand twitched. I pulled my hand back, suddenly.

Brett's eyes were open. Still groggy. I could see the mists of sleep still clouding his brown eyes.

"Who were you talking to?" he asked, his speech quiet and slightly slurred.

"Brett! You're alive."

He grinned, weakly. But sincerely. I felt myself smiling.

"Last time I checked. Yeah."

I felt new tears moisten my eyes, despite how much I forced them to stay back. It wasn't good to cry around Brett. He'd crack a joke about it. And I needed to look tough. He was my fellow hunter, after all.

But despite all that, the tears fell freely down my face. If I was my own officer, I'd have myself flogged. But right now, all I could do was reach out and squeeze his beckoning hand, still semi-motionless on the bed.

In a half-sob, I managed to choke out. "I'm so sorry."

"Why?" he asked, so faint that I wanted to weep. Get a hold of yourself, Kat!

"I should have…I should have fought harder. I shouldn't have let this happen. I wasn't strong enough."

"Kat," he whispered, and squeezed my hand back. "If I'm alive, I'm pretty sure it's because you saved me."

"Cindy…" I started, before he cut me off.

"Cindy can only stitch me back up. You made me want to be saved."

My breath caught in my throat. I couldn't respond. Even Treth was taken aback.

Brett smiled, as his eyes slowly closed.

"Brett?" I almost yelled.

"I'm alive, Kat. But…just…" He yawned. "Sleepy. I'm going to get some extra rest. You go get something to eat. You look like a walking corpse."

"I'm not hungry."

"Go eat. That's an order."

"Who put you in charge?"

He smiled, ever so faintly, as his breathing steadied, and I felt his hand loosen. He looked so peaceful. But, even so, I made sure to check his vitals.

"You're acting like Trudie," Treth said.

"I now understand why," I replied.

"He will pull through. Let's go eat."

I looked at Brett for a few seconds longer, and turned my back, limping slightly out of the hospital room.

"I hate hospital food. But that Chinese place down the road may be good."

"So, you are going to get something to eat?"

I raised my eyebrow, and nodded, hesitantly.

"So, you'll follow my orders?" I could practically feel Treth's childish glee.

258

"When have I not?"

Treth snorted in disbelief so hard that if he had been drinking milk, he could have weaponised it.

I waved my goodbyes to some medical staff that recognised me from my frequent visits and exited into the red-tinged late afternoon exterior of the hospital. Waiting for me, leaning up against the wall underneath a no-smoking sign was Pranish. Smoking.

The incongruity of the scene made me forget about our last encounter. But only briefly.

"Hi," I said, simply, crossing my arms. I wasn't wearing my coat and my bare arms were covered in small plasters.

"Hey," he replied, taking a drag and then putting it out on the wall and tossing the stub into the trashcan. An impressive toss, actually, I might add.

"I didn't know you smoked."

"A new…habit," he replied. He wasn't smiling. And I sensed a hesitance in his mannerisms.

"What caused it?" I asked.

"You, partly."

I snorted. "Don't lay your death stick addiction on me. Trudie started smoking long before I became a stressful burden."

He sighed.

"I know. But…yeah. The stress of you going missing, Trudie still with that…well, that doesn't matter… Colin, the disinheritance. It got a little too much. Trudie got me hooked. Said it would help me relax."

"Does it?"

He shrugged.

I stood facing him for a while, waiting for him to say something. To do something.

"It's good to see you again," he said, finally. And it sounded sincere. "Especially, outside the hospital rather than in it."

I opened my mouth to respond, but he beat me to it.

"I'm sorry, Kat. Sorry for my behaviour. Sorry for blaming you. I've just been so…frustrated. Angry. I thought…I thought that after you killed Andy, that I would have a shot with Trudie. But then she just…"

"She's alive, Pranish. Conrad tracked her to Goldfield."

His eyes widened.

"Are you sure?" he shook his head. "Of course, you are. Conrad is always right. Even when he's wrong."

"He's also an angel."

"I wouldn't go that far."

Both of us managed to maintain a straight face for approximately three seconds. I won't admit who laughed first (I did).

"Rifts, Kat…" Pranish finally said, tears in his eyes from laughing at our bad joke. "I've missed you."

I half-sprinted across the divide between us and hugged my friend tightly.

"I'm sorry, Prani. Sorry for abandoning you guys. Sorry for not being there. Sorry for putting you through all this. All the time. I'm sorry for the late-night drives. The hospital visits. The homework you did for me while I was comatose."

He hesitated hugging me, for a second, and then returned it.

"I came here to apologise. Not to be apologised to. I'm the moron who shouted at you because Trudie decided to run away from home."

"But you were right. I should have been there. For you and her."

"You killed her boyfriend. I understand why you wouldn't want to face her. Even if he was a monster and an asshole, it's hard to explain that to her. Especially to her."

He smiled, sadly.

"It's hard explaining anything to our dear Trudie. She's not stupid. Far from it. But that means she doesn't think she has to listen to anybody else. She knows the right answer already."

I frowned. "But does that mean she knows what she's doing now?"

"In Goldfield?" He considered the question. "I don't know. But…let's find out."

I nodded. "I have no plans to go to Goldfield. At least for now. But I'll see what Conrad unearths."

"She's coming back. I know she will."

I smiled. "I know. And when she does, we'll be here for her."

Like she had been there for me. So many times before. Despite the scolding. Despite the nagging. She had been there for me. And I now understood how painful that must've been for her – yet she did it anyway.

When she finally came back, it would be my turn to be a good friend. I owed her that much. And more.

Chapter 20. Saviour

Brett shivered in the icy, winter air. His t-shirt was not nearly enough to keep out the chill. Yet, he wasn't cold. He didn't feel the bite of frost around him. Or the heat of the now dead fires. He felt nothing on his skin. Not his unshed tears, not his dried sweat, and not the crusted blood.

He stared in the direction of scorched brickwork. But his stare was actually gazing at something else. Something that smelled like blood, faeces and death.

And it sounded…

No…

It screamed.

Men muttered to each other. Brett didn't hear a word. Someone bustled past him. They were carrying a fire hose. Brett had wanted to be a fireman. He recalled that, vaguely. Yesterday, he would have been excited by the red trucks. He would have asked the men in high-visibility jackets a load of questions. So many that his mother would have had to drag him away, sparing the firemen the innocent annoyance of a youth. He would have marvelled at the hydromancers and their control of the fire foam and water.

He would have beamed as only a child could.

But today – he didn't.

He sat, on what used to be a part of his house. In the distance, he saw smoke. The other farm holdings. They hadn't been the only one. A woman tried to speak to him. He didn't reply. He couldn't. He kept his gaze low, when he wasn't looking at the smoky horizon. The lights of a multitude of emergency vehicles leant a visual cacophony to the scene. Brett would have found joy in it the day before.

Now…he felt nothing.

When he did feel something, it was only resentment.

Because they had arrived too late. Because they didn't arrive when it mattered.

And they never could arrive on time. And never would.

Brett ignored a man in a police uniform, and another wearing paramedic gear. They shook their heads and left him alone. They searched the husk of a farmhouse. Brett was not sure why or what for.

Everything of value was dead.

"Emptiness."

The sound of the voice, gruff, almost unkind, scathing, yet…so much deeper…was the only thing to bring Brett's head up. The rising sun silhouetted the man who stood before him. As Brett's eyes adjusted, he could see the man in detail. And the numbers 16 − 1, tattooed in blue ink on his arm.

"Emptiness," the man repeated. "You feel it?"

Brett found himself nodding, before he could even consider the words.

"You will keep feeling it, boy. For all time. Until there really is emptiness. There is a hole in your soul now. A gigantic hole that can never be truly filled. And it seeps a poison that demands an antidote."

"Why?" Brett asked, simply. His voice was hoarse from screaming.

"Why?" the man asked, aghast. "Because the world is a cruel, cruel place. And when someone threatens you with hell, you should only indicate to the world around you. And tell them that you are already there. But…it doesn't have to be that way."

He squatted down and Brett could see him in more detail. His eyes were stern. Almost blank. Like he was a robot. But underneath all that…Brett saw sadness. A hole in his soul. And Brett felt it too.

"Boy…do you want this to happen to other people?"

Fire. Blood. Screams.

They're gone…

"No."

"Do you want revenge, my boy? Against those who have wronged you? Against the monsters that take away little girls. Against the beasts in the night who have left you alone? Do you want the antidote for the poison?"

"Yes."

Brett felt someone place a blanket over his shoulders. The man promptly pulled it off and threw it aside.

"He's a man now," he said. "And a man must feel the cold."

He stood up and offered Brett a hand, pulling him to his feet.

"My name is Rupert Finley. You will call me Finley or sir."

"Yes, sir."

He guided Brett past the now covered corpses of his dead and disembowelled family. There was a body missing. Brett knew it would be. She was the first to go. Into the darkness.

His sister. Taken by blood-drinkers. The same blood-drinkers she had invited into their home.

A black van waited on the corner of the property, beyond the cop cars, useless ambulances, and fire engines. It bore no insignia. It had no sirens. Its windows were blacked out. Finley opened the back of the van. Brett entered, and sat among a group of boys his age. Some were covered in blood and soot. Others had injuries, covered hastily with bandages. All of them had the same, earnest expressions.

One boy looked Brett in the eyes and nodded. He nodded back. They understood each other. More than anyone else ever could.

Finley stood at the back of the van, surveying the haunted passengers.

"Welcome to the Corps," he announced, and closed the doors.

Chapter 21.Conspiracy

The minotaur job had scored us a hefty paycheque. Hefty enough that Cindy dedicated the next week during Brett's recovery to attending to her other business, Guy decided to buy a new bike and Hammond was resentful that he didn't join us in time for such a bounty. Me? I spent the time thinking. I had a lot on my plate. Not just personal stuff, like my confusing feelings for the hospitalised Brett, but all these promises I'd made, and the enemies lurking around the corner.

I had made promises to Duer that we'd find his kinth, to Treth that I'd get him a body, to Candace that I would face the Mentor…and the threat of the ever-elusive Conclave was still out there. Which got me thinking along conspiratorial lines. And while it is never good to make assumptions on such flimsy evidence, I couldn't help but start drawing lines between events and people in my life.

The Conclave had its claws in Digby. It had its claws in Candace, before she went rogue. And it had its claws in Blood Cartel and Jeremiah Cox. And more than all that, it somehow managed to get my freelancer license revoked.

Which suggested that it was powerful. And had a vast network to exploit.

Which got me thinking:

What if Andy had been involved?

I know. A crazy thought. But, hear me out.

His father is a councillor. Which means he's automatic scum. The Garce mansion had been filled with werewolves and had more the feeling of a barracks than a politician's home. Which suggested some sort of paramilitary agenda. Andy had been an alpha of his pack. That much was clear. What wasn't clear was the goal of his pack, besides his laying a claim to me. I was pretty sure that his father was in on it. Councillor Garce was probably a werewolf as well. Perhaps, I'd get to kill him. Not for revenge, though. I didn't feel any sort of personal animosity to the councillor. But a client could buy that animosity if they were so inclined.

Garce was probably just some scumbag politician, but I couldn't help but try to make connections. I was just a bit short of turning a room in Cindy's house into my very own *Beautiful Minds* room. That would be hard to explain to Cindy. The group believed me about the Conclave. Especially Guy and Brett. But tracking down secret societies was not our job. We're monster hunters. If the Conclave sends monsters after us, we'll kill them. It isn't our job to go chasing after them.

While I didn't create a room filled with deranged newspaper clippings connected by pins and threads, I did begin to write down my thoughts in a hardback notebook. I had plenty of time alone at home while Brett recovered, Cindy worked with her magic schools and Guy and Hammond took on freelance jobs. Alone at home being relative, of course. There was still Alex meowing at me for attention, Duer attempting to train the cat as a steed, and Treth trying to give me sage advice that was very likely plagiarised from his master. When Treth was being more sincere, however, he took an interest in my conspiracies.

"The fundamental question is," he said, as I wrote down a list of possible reasons why the Conclave would use Jeremiah Cox, Digby, Blood Cartel and, possibly, Garce. "When you discover more about this Conclave, what are you going to do about it?"

"I don't think there's much I can do about it. If they are coming after us, then I need to know as much about them as possible so we can defend ourselves."

Treth nodded, sombrely. "Why would they target you? It's not like you're actively going after them."

I shrugged. "Candace suggested that it was because I was a discarded asset, like her. They tried to use me to get to her, but after I failed to fulfil their whims, they decided to clip my wings."

"You a bird now?"

"I'm trying to be poetic."

I put down my pen and rubbed my eyes. It was almost dinner time. I'd woken up late and lazed around the house all day before writing in my conspiracy journal.

"I wonder if the Necrolord knows anything more…" Treth pondered.

"*Candace*," I corrected him. She wasn't the Necrolord anymore. She was getting better. I had to believe that. I needed to believe that!

"Candace might know something," he said, a hint of irritation in his voice.

"She might." I nodded. But was she in the right frame of mind to answer my questions?

I opened to a blank page in my notebook and wrote down a question: "Is Councillor Garce a member of the Conclave?"

"How are you going to contact her?" Treth asked. While he complained about the crowded conditions inside my head, he didn't experience Candace's presence, it seemed. And didn't know that Candace could and did often speak to me. But she had to instigate the conversations. Probably her affinity for necromancy. I was the puppet, after all.

"If I call out to her enough, I should get her attention."

"And is this the question you want answered?"

I shrugged. "One of them. But it's the one hunch I have that has very little evidence. If she has anything to say about it, I can scrap it or confirm it."

"Well, then. Go ahead."

I felt his gaze on me, watching me expectantly.

The problem was, I had never really tried to explicitly contact Candace before. Her attention seemed to drift to me at random, or when she felt I was under intense stress. I didn't know if she could sense that I only wanted to chat. Less than that.

I closed my eyes to concentrate but realised that was counter-intuitive. My connection to Candace was through her hazel-coloured eye, after all. Instead, I stared at my written question. Really stared at it. As if trying to burn it with laser vision.

"Candace?" I asked aloud.

Nothing.

I repeated her name.

Still nothing.

"Candace, I need to talk."

The silence in the house was exacerbated by her lack of reply. I paused, considering the question and listening to the distant sound of the night.

Well, if I was the only human who was home.

"CANDACE!" I yelled, startling Treth and even causing Duer to drop something made of glass in the other room.

"What?!" Candace responded, her voice inside my head, sounding like she was speaking through a bad quality microphone. Her voice sounded anxious, as if I had awoken her from a rest. Where could she be where she'd be sleeping around supper time?

I looked at the question, blinking as if to indicate it to her.

"Yes," she said. "I think so. He was at the meeting with the Mentor. Why…"

She must have figured out why it mattered.

"That is something I should have mentioned…"

Candace's presence disappeared as she broke the connection. She must think I'm angry with her. Angry that she hadn't told me that I had yet another connection to the Conclave. That Andy's father was one of her ex-employers.

Admittedly, I was a bit peeved. But I didn't think she'd kept the information from me. She had no reason to do so. If anything, telling me would have convinced me sooner to oppose the Conclave.

No, this was just Candace being absent minded. How could a girl be so precocious and brilliant, yet so incapable of performing basic tasks?

Well, no matter. I had confirmation now.

"Did she say anything?" Treth asked.

"Yes. Garce is a member of the Conclave."

"Congrats, your hunch was correct. All those awful detective jobs have paid off."

"Not at all. If I didn't have Candace's eye, then I'd still just be having baseless suspicions."

"Not going to change my mind on that," he said, stubbornly.

I sighed. "Everyone else doesn't seem to notice anymore."

"That's because they don't believe it's her eye. They think it was just some magic gone haywire."

"That's technically true."

Before Treth could have his turn in one of our famous bouts of banter, I heard a thud on my bedroom window. I stood up in a flash, knocking over my chair. I reached for Voidshot, holstered on my table, and levelled it at my window. Treth had gone silent, his retort forgotten.

There were no additional thuds on the window, but the hammering of my heart was loud enough. I approached the closed curtains, gun ready.

It was probably nothing. But why then wasn't Treth telling me off? He was also anxious. Can you blame us? We deal in horror and have been cooped up alone all day discussing evil secret societies. Of course, we get jumpy on occasion! Especially when the last two things to tap on my window had been demons and vampires. And even if Digby and Terhoff were dead, there were still plenty more things that could go bump in the night. Hopefully they'd die to silver.

I kept Voidshot steady and extended my left hand out towards the white curtains. Treth held his breath. I stopped as I heard scratching. Like an animal. Or a monster. Tap. Tap. Tap on the glass. A claw.

With a flourish, I pulled the curtains aside. Looking up at me, with its head cocked and with large saucepan eyes, unmistakably judging me, was a small brown and white owl.

Bemusement replaced fear.

"Eep!" Duer cried out, as he flew inside to check up on all the hubbub, and then promptly flew out at the sight of the predatory bird.

The owl on the other side of the glass maintained its stare, not even sparing the bite-sized pixie a glance.

"It doesn't look undead," Treth noted.

"Because it isn't. It's an owl."

He sounded offended. "I…I know that. I was just wondering if it was an undead owl."

"Right…" I leaned closer to the glass and the owl maintained eye contact. "It doesn't look demonic or vampiric, either."

I stood up straight and held my arms to my side triumphantly, as if I had just solved a big case.

"This, my dear Treth, is a normal owl."

"What type?"

My pose became less triumphant. I noticed then that the owl had something tied around its neck. A red ribbon, and attached to it, a small note.

I slowly opened the window so as not to startle the bird. It hopped closer to the opening and presented its neck.

"I think you have the wrong house, owlie," I said. "I'm not a wizard."

"That's a pretty forced reference, Kat."

"I didn't even know it was a reference," I answered, reaching out to gently take the note off the eager and increasingly impatient owl. With the note liberated, the owl hopped back on the windowsill and watched.

"Are you wanting me to read it now?"

The owl's unblinking stare was answer enough.

"You're more dutiful than any postal worker I've ever seen."

I unwrapped the note.

"Ms Drummond,

I am in need of your services and would like to meet to discuss a contract. I am waiting at the Ochre Café in Old

Town. I shall wait until 10pm and then send another message."

I read the message aloud, ending off. "Signed: A."

"A?" Treth asked. "Who is A?"

"I have no idea." I looked at the owl, who was still waiting for something. "Who is A, little guy?"

The owl inclined its head, revealing a small brass pendant on its collar. I took a closer look.

"It's a picture of another owl," Treth said. And so it was.

"Yeah, but I think I've seen it somewhere before."

"Somewhere bad?"

"I don't think so."

The owl turned and with a hop and a jump, took to the sky.

I checked the time on my phone. 7pm. I had time to get to the Ochre Café. But best not keep my mysterious client waiting.

I walked purposefully towards my coat.

"You can't really be considering going." Treth stopped me.

"Why not? It's a client. And I haven't eaten yet."

"Last time you went to an address given to you by window, a lot of people died."

"That message was written in blood. And wanted us to go to a secluded warehouse. This one was delivered by a quite attractive owl wearing a red ribbon. And it was definitely not written in blood. Human blood, at least. The ink could be orc blood, now that I think about it. But ink and orc blood are basically the same thing."

Treth shook his head.

"It could be an ambush by the Conclave."

I couldn't help but laugh.

"If the Conclave wanted me dead, I'd be dead. And I know this café. It's pretty popular. They wouldn't ambush me there."

I felt Treth thinking of more reasons why I shouldn't go. I stopped him.

"Cheer up, Treth. It'll be good to get out of the house. I was beginning to get cabin fever."

My coat on, Voidshot holstered discretely, and my knife sheathed even more discretely, I left the house, shouting at Duer to ensure he didn't grow a toadstool circle while I was away.

Chapter 22. Vendettas

The Ochre Café was located just a street away from the bustling night market. It had a warm, almost golden, glow emanating from its windows. But, despite its strategic location, the venue was not as jampacked as I thought it would be. As I entered, drawing stares from the hostess, I noted only five people in the front of the restaurant. Perhaps it was more a day-time joint? I waited at the entrance, trying to catch the attention of my client, whoever they were. Those who looked up didn't seem to take much notice.

"Excuse me, miss." A waitress came over to me. She seemed visibly unnerved. Why? Were my weapons showing? Or was it the scars? My coat hissed a bit.

Oh. That must be it.

"Miss, are you Kat Drummond by any chance?" she asked, stumbling over her words a little.

I tried to smile to put her at ease, but it must have looked like I was just baring my teeth as the waitress's pupils dilated and she took an unconscious step back. I closed my mouth.

"Yes. I am."

"Miss Doe is waiting for you in the back."

Miss Doe? I had an appreciator of the cliched for a client.

I followed the timid waitress up a small flight of stairs into the back of the café. The light was more low-key here, and there were no patrons. No patrons except a woman clothed in a turquoise sweater, sitting by an open window, next to the owl from earlier. Her nose was buried in a red hardcover. The types which don't have the title on the front. The waitress nodded and beat a hasty retreat. A flaming cloak and owl-owning patron must've been too much for her.

I took a step towards my client, and slowly advanced, taking in her features. She had dark brown, almost black, shoulder length curly hair and a pair of thick-rimmed reading glasses. Despite her oversized sweater, she seemed quite slender. Perhaps even athletic.

The owl hooted at my approach and the woman put down her book, looking at me.

No, it can't be.

She didn't smile, rather examining me like I would a sword. She removed her glasses and placed them next to her book.

"By Athena," I whispered aloud.

"What's by me?"

I was, as I rarely ever am, speechless.

I didn't really worship Athena. Nobody half-sane worshipped the Greek gods or, more accurately, immortal sorcerers. But in high school, there was one woman that I admired. I had posters of her. I read all her articles and her books. And when she disappeared from public life, I spent a better part of a year trawling online forums for sightings.

That time was long gone, but I still used her name as an oath. Even now.

Athena squinted, looking at me even more clinically. I felt that piercing gaze as only an old fan could. The judgement felt like venom.

"What's by me?" she repeated. She sounded annoyed, but also genuinely curious.

"Habit," I said, hastily.

She nodded, slowly, and indicated the seat opposite her.

"She's a god?" Treth asked. "Morrígan would send her reeling across the In Between."

I wanted to shush Treth and his insolence but didn't want to risk Athena noticing. I took a seat, being extra careful not to do anything embarrassing – like setting fire to the tablecloth.

"You're a hard girl to find," Athena said, popping an olive into her mouth and then forming a pyramid with her hands. "When I wanted to find you on your city's hunter database, you were apparently expunged from the records. But then, I heard through my kindred that one of their creations was slain by a group called Kat's Crusaders. My uncle's creation…in fact."

"That minotaur had killed hundreds of people. We had to put it down," I said, defensively. Why was I acting like a dumb fangirl? She was just a Hellenic god. I'd defeated much more powerful vampiric gods before. But still, habits were hard to break. And the fact that Athena, goddess of wisdom, heroes and war, was facing me here and now was hard to believe.

I couldn't help but blink rapidly in surprise as Athena laughed. Short, but it sounded sincere.

"I thought the stories about us were common knowledge," she said.

"A bit full of herself, isn't she?" Treth commented. Even more insolently, I might add.

"Poseidon created the minotaur. The first one, on Earth. It was part experimentation – to see if he could – and part childish resentment. The little mortals wouldn't do exactly as he said, so he had to send something to go break their toys. Or bodies, as became the case. Later, a hunter of the day came to slay this beast. I'm proud to say that he came from a city that was my namesake."

"Theseus?"

"I'm glad you remember. I didn't cultivate so many mortal heroes just so they would be forgotten. A hero, like a hunter, only has their legacy. I could not grant them the immortality of my people, but I could at least ensure that they were remembered. Homer helped with that, of course."

I knew a bit about the Olympians and their effect on Earth. I knew that they weren't actually gods, but rather immortals who had been freely able to jump across the In Between. Before the Cataclysm, that is. Nobody could control rifts now. But all that was hearsay. Hearing this now, from the goddess' mouth…I'm very glad that owl tapped on my window.

The waitress, pale as a sheet, arrived with a notepad. She tried to open her mouth, but before she could, Athena ordered.

"The sirloin. Medium rare. And more red wine and olives for the table."

She looked at me. It took me a while to process the prompting before I ordered a burger and chips and a cola to drink. The waitress was visibly relieved to be able to leave the sparsely populated backroom.

Athena looked lost in thought as she swirled the dregs of her wine around the glass.

"We've changed," she said, quietly, as if to herself. "Immortality gives plenty of time to change, of course. Even my disgusting father had calmed down before I went on this never-ending trip. I wonder what he's doing now? Would he have adapted to life on Earth? Or would he have met the same fate as Apollo. That idiot."

I waited, patiently, but also enthralled by her monologue. It wasn't every day that you met Athena.

The waitress arrived with the olives and drinks, shocking Athena out of her reverie.

"Oh, where was I?" she asked. She pulled her hand through her hair.

"Ah, yes. The minotaur. And why it matters that you killed it. You may or may not know that I do not get on with my uncle – Poseidon. He was a capricious man-child. Worse than my father in many ways. At least my father grew out of his phase. Still, he never came to respect mortals like I did…"

"Is she going to give us a job or just prattle on?"

"A job, Mr Spirit? Oh yes, I'm getting to that part."

Treth held his lack of breath and I almost fell off my chair.

"Wait…you can sense Treth?"

"If Treth is the name of your thoroughly unimpressed ghostly companion, then yes. I see him floating above your head. Like a wisp. But his aura is distinctly unwisp like. Yet…"

She narrowed her eyes at the space above my head.

"He's not a ghost, either. Or a spectre."

She looked me in the eyes.

"I can't say I've ever run into a spirit like him before."

I couldn't believe that she could see and hear Treth. Actually, I could. She was Athena! Am I fangirling again?

"How did you come to meet him?" she asked, standing up and holding her hands behind her back, as she examined the space above my head.

"Um…it's a complicated story."

"I died," Treth said, some excitement in his voice. It must be nice to talk to somebody other than me. Not to sell myself short, of course. I think I'm good company. "And as the darkness took me, I felt nothing. And then, I appeared in a house of odd design, as Kat here was battling a ravenous walking corpse."

"I didn't know you'd just died…"

Treth had never told me how recently he had died before becoming tethered to me. Yet, he had seemed so calm. There was very little doubt in my mind that he had saved my life back then.

"Intriguing," Athena muttered, and I felt her hand on my head. Prodding. I normally would have minded, but…you should get the picture.

The waitress halted as she examined the scene. And what a scene it must be. Athena poking the back of my head while waving her other hand in the air as if shooing away insects. Athena glared at the poor server and then took her seat. The waitress delivered our orders and beat a hasty retreat.

"Athena," I said, not believing that I was saying the words. "You have a job for me?"

"Yes…yes. My apologies. Your companion was just a bit…distracting. There's not much that I encounter that I haven't encountered before. A curse of eternity."

She looked about to drift into thought again when Treth cleared his non-existent throat. She looked up.

"Oh yes, the job. Please eat while I give the brief."

I nodded and dug into my burger. It was good. I should bring Brett here.

"When I heard that some mortals unanointed by an Olympian patron had slain a twisted beast of Olympian origin, I was intrigued. And even more so when I realised that it was you who dealt the blow that killed it. I have been reading up on your career, Ms Drummond, and I am impressed. You have slain many monsters in your short time. And, I'm sure that if it was the habit of modern poets to do so, an epic poem would have already been composed about your deeds."

"I'm just a hunter," I said. "It's my job."

"A job that you do most admirably. The slaying of the minotaur rises to the top, of course. My uncle's twisted creatures don't die easily. He builds in all manner of tricky puzzles to allow for their destruction. I could admire his creativity, if it wasn't used for such villainy."

She sighed. "I'm only glad he's not stuck in this realm. It isn't big enough for the both of us. But I digress again. In killing the minotaur, you have proven yourself to me. And that is no easy feat. I have overseen the great heroes of Perseus, Hercules, Odysseus and Jason. More, even. But not for the last few centuries have I cared enough for a mortal to even grant them a bit of my patronage."

She looked down at her cooling steak and half-drunk red wine. Her brow was creased and her mouth set in sad contemplation.

"Until…the Vortex stopped me from going home. Trapped on your planet, I spent what seemed like an age devising a way to get home. Until…until I met him."

There was silence as I waited for her to continue, even neglecting my meal. Finally, she sighed.

"It's painful. And I don't mind telling you, a practical stranger, this honestly. But losing someone is something I think we both understand. But, for us Olympians, it is perhaps more so. For we don't understand it well. Even when Apollo was murdered, I cared little for him. We are rivals. All of us. Jealous of each other's powers. Threatened.

Yet, here on Earth I discovered someone I did not fear. Nor envy. I discovered someone that I came to love, and I didn't believe that I could love anyone more than I loved him. Until we had our child."

She took a long sip of wine, cut off a sliver of steak, and threw it to her owl.

"My child is gone," she said, suddenly. Without warning. She didn't cry, but I felt power in her voice. A primal pain that I could begin to understand, but it would take decades for me to truly absorb. "And I want you to kill the thing responsible."

"I will do what I can," I said. "But…what creature could best you?"

She laughed, without mirth.

"There's a reason that I had mortals do my work for me. We Olympians are deceivers. Yes, we have some power. Many of us had the power to leap across realms before the Vortex. But more than that, we are just long-lived swine toying with people who don't know any better. No…I can't avenge my son. Or his father. I can only seek out a champion who can do it for me. And support them however I can."

I gulped, simultaneously torn between awe of Athena, discomfort at her openness, and my required professionalism as a hunter. My professionalism won.

"What is the target?"

"A necromancer. Your forte. And the reason I reached out to you. In his pursuit of lichdom, he stole away my son and sacrificed him in a dark ritual."

"Do you know if it worked?"

Athena didn't cry, but I saw that she wanted to. Could she cry?

"It did not. The fool killed my son in vain. But...the reason that I'm in Hope City of all places is that I heard he approaches lichdom now. And soon. Thus, I have been searching for a champion to put him down. Before he is too powerful. He has made a lair in the tunnels underneath Old Town. As your reputation suggests, you will know more about what he has infested those tunnels with than me. And that is why I'd like to hire you, and your Crusaders, to slay the fiend. Avenge the only beings I have ever loved. And be the first hero I have blessed since before your wise men became too wise to follow the lead of cosmic tricksters."

"And wouldn't you be a cosmic trickster?" Treth asked.

"Treth!"

"No, it's valid. My relatives tormented this planet for an age. It is only right that we are doubted."

"But you weren't like them!" I almost shouted. "You made heroes. You guided them. You helped to destroy the monsters. It's why we hunters still look to you as a patron."

She waved aside the comment. I didn't let her.

"Athena, I'll take on this mission. I'll be your champion."

"Thank you, Ms Drummond…"

"Please, call me Kat."

"Kat…don't think that I won't honour the new traditions of heroes. Or the old. Do this for me, and your party will be paid a total of $300 000, plus any relics I can muster from my long-dead heroes."

My jaw almost dropped. Not just at the fortune that would put the Crusaders in the same league, if not higher, than Puretide and Drakenbane, but at the promised relics. What had Athena managed to keep? My mouth watered at the idea of holding a weapon or wearing armour of legend.

Athena began digging into her steak. She looked visibly relieved that I accepted the contract. The emotion she had shown before, restrained as it was, had not been in the character known to the world. But because of that, I felt privileged. I'd seen the human in the god. And now I was working for her.

Who could have thought I would go from monster hunter to Athena's champion in one day?

Chapter 23. Into the Darkness

"No! Under no circumstances will I allow you to go gallivanting in the sewers and hunting liches," Cindy yelled at a very sheepish Brett.

He was about to retort with his thoughts on the matter but winced as he tried to lift himself out of his bed. Didn't do well for his case.

He had been discharged from the hospital but was still bedridden. Cindy and the doctor were positive that he'd make a full recovery in time. He'd just need daily doses of healing magic. Not too much, mind you. Too much and the body wouldn't heal right. Like taking triple the prescribed medication. He needed a set amount of healing every day. No more. No less. Luckily, he had Cindy there to provide it, so we didn't have to worry about mounting medical bills. Yeah, we were drowning in cash from that minotaur hunt, but even a lake would eventually be drained if it wasn't topped up.

"Don't worry…" Hammond grinned, snidely. "I'll look after the mad cat for you."

"I can look after myself," I retorted, and leaned closer towards Brett, shoving him back down so he wouldn't hurt himself by getting up. "We can handle this. I've killed mountains of necromancers by myself. And this time I've got a purifier behind me."

"And a pyromancer," Hammond added, desperate for affirmation. Or just wanting to tease Brett.

"No breacher. No explosives expert," Brett responded, allowing me to push him back down without any resistance. My hand hovered over his shoulder. Just in case he wanted to rise again. Really. That's the only reason.

"It's zombies. Not a drake or vampire cartel," Guy added. "Personally, I think Kat is being generous letting us take a cut."

I frowned. It wasn't that simple. Liches, even only half-turned liches, were not just some simple undead. They were powerful physical manifestations of necromancy and corruption. Often, they resembled wights, apparently. I'd never seen one. But that was about to change.

I didn't voice my concern, however. I didn't want Brett to do something stupid.

"Buddy, I know it's not nice to hear," Guy said. "But I don't think we're needed on this mission. Kat's right. One-armed McGee, as well. With Cindy on healing and purification, any sort of dark magic they throw our way will be mitigated. And hate to say it – but fire is better than bullets this time around. And, besides…"

He looked my way.

"We've got her."

"Is that a compliment, Mr Ndebe?" I sniggered. Brett's lips curved upward into a smile. Victory!

"I don't know why we're trying to convince you." Cindy sighed. "I'm not letting you out of bed regardless."

"Fine!" Brett said, but I didn't sense any sort of resignation in his voice. We'd better wrap up the mission quickly before he did something stupid.

"Great. Now that your machismo can be ignored, let's get to the plan. Feel free to give feedback. You're still a part of the team," Cindy said, accepting Brett's apparent resignation.

The group turned to me. Despite Cindy's name being on the registry, they all seemed to think I was the leader. I preferred to think of the Crusaders as organised chaos. But if they were looking to me for laying down the ground work, then so be it.

"Cindy, what do you know about liches?"

She shook her head. "Not much, Kat. Not my speciality. Just that they're super undead necromancers."

I resisted sighing. We'd have to rely on my limited knowledge. And Treth's. But I sensed that Treth's knowledge may not be that limited. Just painful.

"Athena claims that this man is in transition to becoming a lich. That can mean many things. For prudence sake, let's assume the worst. First, some basic lore. Liches are undead. Essentially. Which means that purification will work, to a point. Most liches tend to emit a corruption aura powerful enough to rebound most purification spells. Which means…"

"Fire," Hammond interjected.

I nodded. "And swords. But it may not be that simple. Depending on what phase of his transformation he is in, he may already have a phylactery."

"Phylactery?" Brett asked.

"An object of some magical importance. It can resemble many things. A spell book, an enchanted amulet, a jar containing a soul…The form matters less than the function. The lich uses the phylactery to contain his mortal essence, tethering it to this realm and granting himself immortality."

"Zombies and wights are also immortal, Kat. What makes a lich special?" Hammond asked. You'd think a Puretide operative would be more knowledgeable about the dark emperor of undead.

"Zombies and wights are under constant threat of compulsion by a necromancer. And while they don't actively rot, they do have a problem with regenerating their lost limbs. If a wight loses an arm, it relies on a necromancer to stitch it back on and tether it back to the host corpse. Necromancers and wights don't like this symbiotic relationship. Necromancers want complete dominance and wights tend to want independence. For a necromancer who wants the immortality of undeath, independence from another necromancer, and dominance over the undead, becoming a lich is an ultimate goal."

"Why don't more necromancers do it, then?" Guy asked.

"It costs too much," Treth said, sternly. I repeated his words. Guy didn't look satisfied but didn't press.

"So, to summarise," I continued. "The lich may have the following powers: corruption and necromantic powers, regeneration of limbs that even silver cannot stop, a force-field that rebounds purification magic, and the ability to take

300

control of any undead instantly. This includes reanimating at whim, without the need for spell-words."

"What?!" Cindy was particularly shocked by the last part.

I nodded, morosely.

"The research shows that liches have an ability to raise the undead as if they were sorcerers. No need for channelling. No need for spell-words. It's as if they gain a spark that is attuned to necromancy."

Cindy leaned forward, clasping her hands and thinking deeply.

"Demanzite shot," Guy offered. "We've got some stocked."

"That stuff is illegal," Hammond said, narrowing his eyes.

"So is burning your exes house down for cheating on you. Didn't stop you."

Hammond was open-mouthed for a few moments before slumping back into his chair. Under his breath, he whispered.

"She took my cat…"

"Kat," Brett looked at me from his prone position. "What's the plan?"

Sheez! Way to pressure someone.

"To reliably kill the lich," I said. "We must destroy his phylactery."

"Assuming he has one already."

"Assume the worst. So, my proposal is to target his phylactery. If it is destroyed, he will either die or become vulnerable to any of our attacks. I'm not scared of his horde, but any of us could make a mistake. I advise that we sneak past as many of his corpses as we can, until we positively identify the phylactery."

"How will we do that?" Cindy asked.

"Duer," I answered. "Pixies can sense dark weylines better than any human can. Phylacteries put out a thick dark strand of weyline. Duer will track it down and we'll destroy it."

"What am I doing?" Duer squeaked, flying into the room. He had tagged along to Brett and Guy's apartment, and immediately was drawn to fixing their neglected plants.

"You're gonna help kill a lich."

"Neat," he replied, and flew off again.

"Where do I fit into this?" Hammond asked, looking somewhat dejected that the thrust of the plan rested on a bite-sized fae.

"Where you always fit in," Brett replied. "Shoot fire till you get drowsy and then take a nap."

"Fine by me." He shrugged, despite Brett's attempted provocation. I knew that Hammond was a powerful sorcerer. I'd never actually seen his spark tire. He knew this as well, so he didn't feel the need to get defensive. For a sorcerer, he was actually pretty laid-back. Never ever uttered the word *husk* or insist on better treatment because he was arbitrarily born with a bit of vortex dust inside his soul.

"Cindy," I said, turning to her. She awoke from her preoccupation and looked at me. "You may need to take a hard role. We may need healing and purification attacks. A mass de-animation, even. If we get swamped. Are you up for it?"

I'd seen Cindy's mouth coated in vomit after de-animating hordes of undead without rest, while sending purification bolt after purification bolt at the enemy. She'd looked like the walking dead herself.

She nodded.

I stood up, and the others (with the exception of Brett) did the same.

"We're on a tight deadline. Every hour we wait, he may be getting stronger. We have the place. We have a plan."

I looked at my motley crew. Willing to lay down their lives to put a monster in the ground and get a more than passable bounty out of it.

"Let's go slay a lich!"

Chapter 24. Death

We had stocked up on energy drinks, some magic infused food bars and some snacks before heading out. We had no idea how long we would be in these tunnels. And best to be prepared. Waiting outside the towering entrance to Hope City's abandoned sewers, I chugged down the last of my coffee. It had already been a long night. I didn't want to leave Athena waiting. And the lich could be growing in power as we waited for another day. No, we had to put it down tonight.

My cell phone's clock read 1am. Usual time for me to be out and about. Early, in fact.

I cricked my neck and did a few stretches.

"Careful going in, Kat," Treth warned me. It was nice to have him nagging again. I preferred it to his melancholy moments. "Undead we've dealt with. But liches are a different game entirely."

I nodded to him, subtly, so Duer wouldn't notice. My pixie roommate was currently stationed in my tactical vest pocket, underneath my flaming coat. He wanted to be in on the action, slitting zombie throats (for all the good that'd do!), but I managed to convince him that he'd be most useful directing me to the phylactery from my pocket.

I felt a hand on my shoulder. I looked up to see Cindy's face, obscured by the darkness.

"We're all going to come out of this, this time," she said. "And not injured. I want no casualties. I won't allow casualties! That's a promise."

I nodded. Cindy had taken Brett's injuries hard. I don't know why. I'm the one who wasn't able to give him effective first aid.

Hammond took a final puff of his cigarette, threw it to the ground and stomped on it. If he had both his arms, I'm sure he would have cracked his knuckles.

"Let's get this party started," he said, and took point.

Side by side, two sorcerers, two fighters and a pixie entered the darkness of long forgotten infrastructure. I was glad it was forgotten, however. An abandoned sewer was always preferable to a sewer in use.

We proceeded without the use of our flashlights until it was too dark to see, and we each turned our lights on. Undead often didn't care about the darkness, so we would only be inhibiting ourselves if we didn't turn on some lights.

We trudged along in the cold confines of this stone tunnel for ages. Duer was on standby. He'd only talk when he sensed something. At the entrance, he had reported a generally dark weyline, but not much else.

We walked through the dark tunnels, taking random turns. We walked for so long that Hammond abruptly stopped.

"Are we really…"

I shushed him and took point, holding my finger to his lips.

Footsteps. No. Metal boot-steps. And the scraping of metal on metal. And most importantly, groans. In the distance.

"Undead," I whispered. That shut him up.

We moved towards the sounds, monitoring our footfalls and moving as softly as possible. Instead of just being anxious about the sounds I was making, I found myself becoming increasingly anxious about everyone else's sounds.

I definitely needed to learn more about working in a team. But solo-hunting habits die hard.

Even before the source of the sounds came into view, Duer spoke softly.

"I sense a strand. My kinth, it smells horrible!"

"What direction?" I asked quietly.

"Keep headin' this way."

Well, where there's zombie groans, there are probably necromancers and liches.

I was not exactly right. I was the one to peek around the corner, revealing a group of shambling undead. But they weren't just zombies. Over their pale, rotten flesh, were grafted on metal sheets. On almost every part of their body! Only some sections were allowed to breathe in between. And not only were these modified undead – abhorrent – armoured, they were also armed. Their fragile human hands had been replaced with machete blades.

Their necromancer meant business. They were more suited to fighting than Jeremiah Cox's abhorrent. If possible, I wouldn't want to fight them. I didn't think I could kill them as seamlessly as I did zombies.

I whispered to the group.

"About five abhorrent. Well-armed. Sneak past them to the other side. We don't have to fight them."

I turned back and took one final look at the shambling group of metal-wearing undead. I willed my coat to dull its glow, and I memorised the path across to the other side of the tunnel, where Duer said the strand of darkness pointed.

I took a silent breath and dashed as quietly as a wraith across the gap to the other side. I heard no growls, roars or hurried metal-clanging. Relieved, I flashed my flashlight to signal for Cindy to cross. She did so. Guy was next. And lastly, Hammond.

Hammond was just to us, and was as quiet as the rest of us, when I heard the all too familiar bellow of an undead's war cry. The beasts hissed and growled as they charged, their metal-clad feet clanging on the stone floors. Hammond turned on the beasts and let loose a wave of fire. Some caught alight, immediately creating the overwhelming stench of toasted flesh, but kept charging. He blasted them again. And again. Until there was only one left advancing, crawling along the ground, its flesh blistering and bubbling between its metal-plates. I put my foot on its head and slashed its neck with both my blades. My swords sailed through its flesh like melted butter.

"I see you're taking your role seriously," Guy commented to Hammond, out-loud. It seems our cover was blown, so no point being quiet anymore.

"Magic alarm," Cindy said. "I'm sure of it. Just happened to trip only then."

"No use arguing over who tripped what," I said. The bellows of what could have been a hundred undead backed up my statement. "No more sneaking. Let's run."

We bolted down the tunnels, turning our lights on full blast. A few zombies blocked our way, but I dispatched them easily. They weren't the armoured abhorrent. Duer suddenly called out different directions, causing us to twist and turn down dark tunnels. Zombies and abhorrent spotted us from behind and gave chase, screeching, roaring, groaning and demanding a bite of all of us.

"Right!" Duer called, and we turned, just to face a sea of sickly yellow eyes, reflecting the light of our flashlights. They charged, so rapidly that their combined stench pushed forward like a tidal wave. Guy opened fire with his machine-pistols, but the bullets either plinked into the armour or harmlessly thudded into exposed flesh.

My peripheral vision was lit up by flaming orange, as Hammond let loose a barrage of fire at our pursuers.

"I'll hold them off!" he yelled. "Go!"

We complied, not for a second thinking Hammond was planning on sacrificing himself for us. If we were out of range, he could release the full extent of his fiery power.

I charged forward, meeting a zombie face to face, before I removed said face from its body. The head sailed through the air, squelching as it hit the wall. I followed through with the skewering of another zombie, beheading it with my other sword.

Guy gave up trying to shoot at the creatures and pushed through with his dagger. Cindy shot a purification bolt, spitting a creature in the head and causing it to de-animate.

I swung my sword in a wide arc, disembowelling another zombie until...

Clank!

My body erupted in shivers as the force of metal impacting metal sent vibrations up my arm. The abhorrent seemed to grin madly with a mouthful of metal capped and sharpened teeth. It brought its machete arm down on me. Or it would have if Duer hadn't flown out and stuck a sewing needle in its eye. Blackened blood sprayed as Duer dodged its flailing. I aimed carefully for its neck and swung. At least its neck was vulnerable.

"This way!" Duer called, flying down the tunnels and acting as our golden guide.

"Go!" Hammond shouted again.

The three of us, following Duer, burst through the undead mob. As we passed a corner, the tunnel lit up and I heard a kaboom. The scent of burning flesh dominated the tunnels.

Keeping up with Duer was hard, as the pixie swooped underneath undead, flew over them, and darted around corners. He was like a bloodhound who had lost track of everything but its prey.

We skidded to a halt as a wall of armoured abhorrent blocked our path. Like a bowling ball against pins, a fireball was lobbed over our heads, knocking the abhorrent to the ground and incinerating them. We ran over their bodies with Hammond who had now caught up.

We heard the distinctly undead noises of rage in the distance, but not close. I was preparing for a few moments of respite when...

"Behind this door," Duer said, ominously. His golden aura flickered, nervously.

I gulped. This would be it. The final boss fight. I just hoped Hammond's spark would hold up.

To allay my concerns, Hammond shoved his way in front and released a concentrated blast of fire, knocking the door off its hinges. So much for respite!

Instinct caused me to charge forward into the room, but an even stronger instinct caused me to stop.

The room was dome-shaped, cluttered with bookshelves, desks, worktables and laboratory equipment. In the centre was a ritual circle. And, hovering a foot above the ground of said ritual circle was not a man, an undead nor a monstrosity. It was all three. Its pale skin was not pale enough to be white, but too pale to be any sort of living flesh colour. Its body was too long, with its spine stretching unnaturally into the air. It was wreathed in a writhing darkness, pulsating and dripping menace and oil-like goo onto the ground, that dissipated into smoke. And on top of all that, its head was stuck between the painful expression of life and death, with half the man's face being alive and screaming, and the other a thin-skin covered skull.

"Kill it!" Treth shouted, with hatred and absolute terror melding at once in his voice.

I charged forward, breaking the others out of their stupor. But it was too late. The man-side of the face receded and became symmetrical with the monstrous, thinly-covered skull. A spark of cold, ice blue sparked inside hollow eyes. His expression, previously frozen in pain, twisted into a smile that tore his face in two.

He held up his palm, and a spear of blackness erupted. Shooting right towards me.

Duer cried out. And I felt the wind knocked out of me as Guy pulled me to the ground.

"Brett wouldn't forgive me…" he began but stopped to pant.

Hammond, reliable as always, stepped forward and released a solid wall of flame towards the lich, just over Guy and my heads. The intense heat already caused sweat to coat my body.

Cindy advanced into the room but turned back.

"Undead!" she yelled. And I heard them. A cacophony of demented cries. Too many for us to handle. And nowhere else to run.

Guy rolled away from me, holstering his pistols and drawing Brett's shotgun. He charged forward to cover, letting the wall shelter his approach.

I pulled myself up. Duer was floating next to me, his face wracked with concern.

"Duer…" I panted. "Where's the phylactery?"

"Dodge!" Treth ordered, and I dove towards one of the work-tables, currently dominated by a dismembered arm. A rod of blackness stuck into the ground where I had been crouched. After a few moments, it dissipated into a puff of smoke.

"Behind the beastie!" Duer yelled, over the cacophony of undead roars, gunfire and incineration.

I peeked my head over the desk. There was a foot-locker behind the lich. At least he hadn't hidden it!

The onslaught of Hammond's fire dissipated as he turned to face the hordes behind us. He tried to launch flames towards the lich and the horde but, with only one arm, that was pretty hard. Cindy was chanting, reading the spells off her scarred arms by tracing her fingers over them. When she got the spell off, we'd have some time, but she'd need time to get if off.

"Guy!" I shouted and signed towards the lich. He nodded.

"Don't do anything stupid," Treth said.

Too late for that.

I took cover. Closed my eyes for a second. And opened them.

I vaulted over the work-bench, knocking the dead arm to the ground and skidding towards the lich. It released a dark javelin towards me, missing me by a hairsbreadth and causing my flaming coat to ignite in irritation.

Zombies closed the gap and Cindy had to break off her chanting to open fire on them with point-blank shots from a sawed-off shotgun. Guy rounded the dome-shaped room. And I…

I charged towards death.

Guy turned over one of the desks to provide cover, and levelled Brett's shotgun at the lich.

Just a gap between us. I saw the blackness pool in the lich's hand. Its sickening grin never abated. Whatever was still human in there was probably enjoying this. I'd make sure to try enjoying killing him.

The black formed into a shard. I vaulted over another table and leapt through the air. The blackness almost escaped the lich's hand, when a puff of silvery powder hit it, shredding skin. The blackness dissipated and the lich's smile wavered.

I took its head off in mid-air, before landing with a knee-shaking thud on the other side, black blood staining my blades before hissing into smoke.

The floating, elongated body didn't collapse. It continued floating, as the flesh and bone around its neck began to knit together, reforming its head. It was regenerating faster than any vampire I'd fought! He truly was a lich.

Duer flew to my side and perched himself on my shoulder.

"In there! The dark stench is coming from there."

I was in luck, as the padlock on the footlocker was open. The lich must've been using it just before we arrived. But I needed to be quick.

I opened the footlocker and my heart sank. It was filled to the brim with what could only be described as clutter.

Random widgets. Useless miniature sculptures. The type of stuff you buy at a tourist trap.

"Which one is it?!"

Duer didn't answer. He was looking wide-eyed at the entrance, as Cindy and Hammond had been pushed back by a group of heavily armoured abhorrent that towered above them. Cindy had a wide cut across her cheek, but was still fighting, sending purification bolts through the undead.

I turned towards the lich, towering above me. Its lower-half had grown back fully, revealing a bottom row of grinning teeth. Its skull was reforming already.

I started pulling stuff out of the locker, trying to sense evilness and smashing what I could on the ground. The lich rotated to face me. The flames where its eyes should be flickered to life. Guy fired another demanzite shot, just to have the powder dissipate on a wall of blackness.

"Duer! Treth! What do I do?!"

The lich raised its hand. I kept turfing out clutter, destroying everything. But it wasn't working. The liches head was fully back. And it winked at me…

An explosion wracked the dome and the lich turned its head.

The abhorrent lay prostrate all over the floor, their limbs scattered. Cindy and Hammond stood, just as stunned as the rest of us, as Brett jogged through (with only a slight limp), carrying a bandolier of grenades.

"Katty!" he yelled, and tossed a grenade to me, sailing past the lich and landing in my hand. I pulled the pin and shoved it in the box. We should have thought about this the first time.

I dove for cover behind a metal desk in the far corner of the room, just as the lich regained its senses and its smile twisted into a frown.

Boom.

Widgets and pieces of twisted metal from the footlocker impacted all around the dome, rending through anything not made of metal or stone. I kept my head down, covering Duer with my hands and feeling every bang as pieces of shrapnel impacted with my cover.

And as rapidly as it had begun, it stopped. I peeked over the top, and my mouth dropped.

The lich, its profile facing me, was still floating. It hadn't worked!

It twisted its head, with audible creaking, and I saw the other side of its face. The blue fire had spread. The creature collapsed to the ground, as its own fire began to incinerate it, and its flesh started to fall in on itself. Rapidly. Its head caved in, then its rib-cage, and its arms twisted like tortured insects, finally dissipating into the fog-like darkness, pooled onto the floor like a puddle. Cindy walked towards it and clicked her fingers. Gold erupted from her and the blackness went up in smoke.

It was over.

My body almost collapsed from the palpable relief. We had done it! We'd slayed the lich. Athena had her vengeance. And…and…

We were all rich!

Glowing the most golden I'd ever seen him, Duer flew out towards Brett, who was now leaning on Hammond, as Cindy marched towards him with an expression that would put out forest fires.

I could only smile. The sort of smile that comes after a job well done, and the relief that you weren't going to die. Just yet, at least.

"Oy, Brett," I called.

He turned to me, with a beam on his face, which soon wilted. The others looked my way and their faces turned to horror.

"Kat…"

What was with them? We'd won.

I turned around.

And I saw a crack.

A crack in the air. And inside it…the In Between.

"Rift!" Cindy shouted.

I tried to take a step forward, but my body didn't move. I felt the suction on my back. Too hard. A vacuum. And suddenly, it pulled me backwards.

"Kat!" Brett screamed. Duer, no longer shining his brilliant gold, flew towards me as fast as his little wings could carry him. I grabbed onto a chair. But it gave way. And was pulled with me into the abyss.

Brett's face was red, and he was yelling. Guy and Hammond were holding him back. There was nothing he could do. Nothing any of us could do. Cindy only held her hands over her mouth, tears cascading down her face.

My back hit resistance, and I started to lose feeling in my toes, feet, legs. I was being sucked in. Brett hit Guy in the face and Hammond lost his grip. He clawed his way towards me. Closer, closer.

I reached out my hand.

And he almost got to me.

Almost.

And then I felt…

Nothing.

Chapter 25. Life

There comes a time in life when one wonders if one is truly alive. Brett didn't wonder. He didn't think he was alive at all. He was stuck in a faded world of grey, and he truly believed that he had died alongside his family. Everything since then…it had been a dream.

Which made this a dream.

If only…

He would take any nightmare over this. Anything. And if he wasn't dead yet. He would take death.

A pale young woman with black hair lay prostrate before him. Her head had been separated from her body. He held the blade that did it. Because he had done it. Yet, could he have done it?

When he was already dead.

Because Brett never would have done this. He couldn't have. He never would have killed his sister. No matter how many people she had killed. No matter that she was a vampire. No matter that it was his job. No. His reason. His purpose.

Brett couldn't have done it.

But he had.

"She's gone," Brett murmured. His fellow Corpsmen ignored him, out of respect and confusion, as he knelt next to the vampire murderess. He had muttered the same line over and over. His comrades were used to it by now as they carried other vampire corpses outside, to be eliminated by the sun.

"She's…" Brett stopped as he felt a hand on his shoulder. He looked up to his commander. Finley. His mentor. His only…that didn't matter.

"There'll be others, Callahan."

Other who? Other vampires? Other sisters? No. She was gone. She was dead. There was no more point.

"How?" Brett asked, sobs choking his words.

"Because you're still alive…"

Alive.

"I don't feel alive…"

"None of us does. But we are. And you know how I know this?"

Finley squatted down and looked Brett in the eyes.

"Because we're here. And we're still fighting. Ourselves. Them. The world. And because we've felt alive before. And perhaps, we fight because it reminds us we're alive. That we can still do something."

"She was…everything…"

"No," Finley said, and pulled Brett into his shoulder.

"She wasn't you."

Brett let himself cry then, as his commander held him. His sister lay dead. His knife was bloodied.

"There'll be others, my boy. There is always a reason to keep on living. To keep on fighting. To show this world that it can't keep us down. Not now. Not ever. And when you realise that…you won't need the Corps. Or me. And you won't need her anymore. Just you, Brett. Just you."

***

Just me.

Afterword

Kat's story isn't done yet. While the Necrolord arc is done, the Conclave is still out there, and now Kat has bigger things to worry about. Like what's on the other side of this rift.

This book establishes three things that need to be done in the Post-Necrolord arc. Let's see if you can guess what they are. After they are done, the arc will be complete, and another arc will begin.

I plan for the Kat Drummond Series to go on for quite a while. Not just because more books make a series more financially viable, but also because I'm enjoying writing it.

I hope you have enjoyed reading it so far and I hope to see you in the next book!

Sincerely,

Nicholas Woode-Smith

Acknowledgements

In no particular order, I would like to thank the following people for helping make this book a reality.

Shelley Woode-Smith for providing her proofreading talents. Chelsea Murphy for her extensive feedback and beta reading. All the active members of my ARC list, for ensuring that no error remains (hopefully!) and that the book launches with honest and positive social proof.

And finally: thank you to the readers who have got this far and continue to help make Kat Drummond's universe a vibrant and successful urban fantasy series! Without the reader, the book is just some digital chaff on the internet. So, thank you!

Made in the USA
Middletown, DE
24 April 2021